NEW DIRECTIONS 36

*In memoriam*

ROBERT LOWELL
1917–1977

VLADIMIR NABOKOV
1899–1977

# N D

## New Directions in Prose and Poetry 36

**Edited by J. Laughlin**

with Peter Glassgold and Frederick R. Martin

 **A New Directions Book**

ACKNOWLEDGMENTS

Grateful acknowledgment is made to the editors and publishers of books and magazines where some of the selections in this volume first appeared: for Allen Ginsberg, *Mind Breaths, Poems 1972–1977* (City Lights Books, Inc.), *River Styx*, and *A Shot in the Street* (Copyright © 1977, 1978 by Allen Ginsberg); for James Purdy, *Contact II* (Copyright © 1977 by James Purdy).

Selections from Delmore Schwartz's verse journals appear courtesy of the Collection of American Literature, Beinecke Library, Yale University.

Breyten Breytenbach's "Five Poems" appear here by arrangement with Meulenhoff Nederland, Amsterdam.

Manufactured in the United States of America
First published clothbound (ISBN: 0–8112–0672–6) and as New Directions Paperbook 449 (ISBN: 0–8112–0673–4) in 1978
Published simultaneously in Canada by McClelland & Stewart, Ltd.

New Directions Books are published for James Laughlin
by New Directions Publishing Corporation,
333 Sixth Avenue, New York 10014

# CONTENTS

# "DON'T GROW OLD"

Six Poems

ALLEN GINSBERG

I
Old Poet, Poetry's final subject glimmers months ahead
What do I want of you at last
Acknowledge the lies of our newspaper world?
Vanity tricked us into anger—shouts, insults?
Now tender mornings, sleep without pain, Paterson roofs white
    snowcovered
Vastness
Sky over City Hall tower and Eastside Park's grass terraces & tennis
    courts
Parts of ourselves gone, sister Rose's apartments, brown corridor'd
    high schools, war years
invisible to ourselves
Too tired to go out for a walk, too tired to end the war
Too tired to save body
too tired to be heroic
The real close at hand as the Stomach
liver pancreas rib
Coughing up gastric saliva
Marriages vanished in a cough
Hard to get up from the easy chair

Hands white   feet speckled a blue toe    stomach big   breasts
     hanging thin
hair white on the chest
too tired to take off shoes and black sox


## II

He'll see no more Times Square
honkytonk movie marquees, bus stations at midnight
Nor the orange sun ball
rising thru treetops east toward New York's skyline
His velvet armchair facing the window will be empty
He won't see the moon over house roofs
or sky over Paterson's streets.


## III

Wasted arms, feeble knees
     80 years old, hair thin and white
          cheek bonier than I'd remembered—
head bowed on his neck, eyes opened
     now and then, he listened—
    I read my father Wordsworth's *Intimations of Mortality:*
". . . trailing clouds of glory do we come
     from God, who is our home . . ."
          "That's beautiful," he said, "but it's not true."

"When I was a boy, we had a house
     on Boyd Street, Newark—the backyard
          was a big empty lot full of bushes and tall grass.
    I always wondered what was behind those trees.
When I grew older, I walked around the block,
     and found out what was back there—
         it was a glue factory."

IV
Will that happen to me?
Of course, it'll happen to thee.

Will my arms wither away?
Yes yr arm hair will turn grey.

Will my knees grow weak & collapse?
Your knees will need crutches perhaps.

Will my chest get thin?
Your breasts will be hanging skin.

Where will go—my teeth?
You'll keep the ones beneath.

What'll happen to my bones?
They'll get mixed up with the stones.


V
Near the Scrap Yard my Father'll be Buried
Near Newark Airport my father'll be
Under a Winston Cigarette sign buried
On Exit 14 Turnpike NJ South
Through the tollgate Service Road 1 my father buried
Past Merchants Refrigerating concrete on the cattailed marshes
past the Budweiser Anheuser-Busch brick brewery
in B'nai Israel Cemetery behind a green painted iron fence
where there used to be a paint factory and farms
where Pennick makes chemicals now
under the Penn Central power Station
transformers & wires, at the borderline
between Elizabeth and Newark, next to Aunt Rose
Gaidemack, near Uncle Harry Meltzer
one grave over from Abe's wife Anna my Father'll be buried.

VI
What's to be done about Death?
Nothing, nothing
Stop going to school No. 6 in 1937?
Freeze time tonight, with a headache, at quarter to 2 A.M.?
Not go to Father's funeral tomorrow morn?
Not go back to Naropa    teach Buddhist poetics a summer?
Not be buried in the cemetery near Newark Airport some day?

# ANOTHER MINOTAUR

PAUL WEST

1

Almost too fatigued to notice the stench of blood and decomposing corpses on the low-lying island, the Japanese troops dug in as best they could in shell-holes that adjoined the salt mud. Threading his way between trios of inert soldiers, Lt. He-Setsu sent a four-man patrol to check if the enemy dead really were dead (and if not so to make them so). As a couple of shots rang out a hundred yards away, he nodded with world-weary neatness, sheathed his sword as if at a signal, and marveled how the blade in catching the sunset had actually seemed to slice light. In the sound of the evening tide he heard a broken *samisen*, rattling like a loose spring in a lacquered box. The nauseating air he breathed in little quanta, thinking his breaths cone-shaped. On his lips, two salts overlay the brown scum that rimmed the sunbaked skin. A reconnaissance plane with red rising sun insignia buzzed the beach and swerved left across the island. Flies made a confetti on his face as he yearned for cherry blossom or bean curd. The patrol came back, trophyless. The wind strengthened while he gnawed hard biscuit, and something, a fluid on his face, seemed to curdle and dry. He thought of a porno song he'd heard once in a night club, *I have sipped the black fluid of my mother*, but willed the refrain away. Into its place fell some gruesome sense of *déjà vu*, as if he had only an hour to live, in a scowl-eyed panic, with his neglected teeth beginning suddenly to ache. Then a low, early moon making pseudodaylight lulled him. He flinched from his trance only a moment later, rapped out a series of orders, appointed sentries, and for the first time sat, on a hillock draped with seaweed. Five minutes' march away, a flag caught his eye; then, toward the central bulge, a lick of sunset on the ridge where observation posts had already been set up. Chilled he rubbed his pecked-looking hands together. He longed for his son, prude that the youth was, and his wife, the ever-wet, the one mincing, the other appetizingly disgraceful, with ever-hard nipples (which she pressed even against strangers while talking, like twin stethoscopes). Dragging off his cap as if tearing away a wreath, he smelled it, curled his nostrils in rebuke at the musky sweatband, and clapped the thing back on. For a while he half dreamed. A soldier brought him a small animal live, but with a shrapnel wound. It was a baby anoa, a species of small buffalo, horns just budding.

"Cook it," he ordered unthinkingly. "No. Cut it up and eat it raw." Why wasn't it yelping? He dreamed again, took *sake* from his silver hip flask, and stood erect to make water for only the second time that day.

Then he heard it, a curt aerial scuffle above the sea but not of the sea. As if an animal had scampered over. Or a very distant aircraft had dived and pulled out. It was the blood in his temples, he thought. Some trick of the humidity affecting his ears. Permafrost of the emotions cracking. It didn't come again, not for several minutes, which he timed with his filth-caked watch. Foreboding he had known, before hitting a beach or when summoned before his colonel; but this intuition of doom reminded him of something half delicious: bathing alone in hot water before returning to the university from his home town thirty miles away. At such times a desolating osmosis had made him shiver, turned his stomach into a jellyfish, and set his teeth on edge. Reverse nostalgia he called it, noting how loose a description that was. After all, despite his buried cravings for *samurai* grandeur, he was only going a short train journey to resume the study of economics. Nothing fierce. He was an A student, a fast study, a natural paraphrast of difficult books, and a lucrative career awaited him. Or it had. Now he had two decorations and a battle scar on his forearm, where a small shell fragment had skimmed through the flesh on its way to a sergeant's throat. He could still taste the sideways spurt of the other man's blood, like fluid smoke. How fared the unburied seargeant now, he wondered. The bulbous lips? The brawny trunk? Humidity increased as night fell, quietening his men as they squatted or half sprawled. Raw flesh for a few, combat biscuit of rice flour for most, had only made them hungrier, reviving a forgotten taste for ordinary food. Indistinctly he wanted to do more for them, have them fish in the shallows or equip them with a tub of steaming rice, but he was as tired as they. Even as the moonlight brimmed complete soon after midnight, and no attack began, he could not sleep, but peered horizontally along the beach at the sandbag forms of the men, a gleam of metal, a hand flashing pale as it rose to an insect bite and fell again. It was almost as if, along the shore of the island, broad pipes had been strewn about for placement in the earth tomorrow; all he saw was tubular, smooth angles bulging from the sand. He longed to step into the water, even if only to unstick and restick his baggy pants and short-sleeved shirt to his crawling skin. Lt. He-Setsu drifted, his mind a parasol borne by an offshore breeze through an immaculate temple garden with stone lions and bridges with concave lintels.

At the first shriek he hardly moved, musing on children at play in speckled blouses; but, as a multiple howl of mingled pain and revulsion cut the humming air, he jerked upright, dizzy and ashake. He could see nothing where the sounds came from, only a complex writhing in the gloam. An erect figure fell, leapt up again, then snapped down. Someone ran, he himself, but sprawled headlong over a body. As his gaze registered, in the moonlight that was not light, he barked a command. Now the beach seemed spread with logs or railroad timber, most of it on the move with lengthwise plunges that veered to one side or the other. Then he saw something like a lid, as of a camouflaged foxhole, lift slowly up into the fan of light and much faster fall. A word cried aloud told him what he could not believe even as his numbed brain made sense, believed, and found the same word: crocodile.

Not one, however, nor a few, but scores of them were lumbering out of the mud, up the beach, and into the lines of overcrowded men. The only firing was spasmodic. Long gurglings came with insensate babble. Men ran and toppled as if over trip-wires. A leg spun up and stayed at a weird angle as if its owner were handstanding. Then it vanished. A thump hit He-Setsu's boot, but as he recoiled he could see only the hillock and a receding tapered tail.

He had not moved in half a minute, nor did he unroot himself as the moon came on strong. The beach writhed as the men ran into one another trying to get inland, only to run into another flock of men from the other side of the island, at this point only three hundred yards wide. The only way off the low promontory was to the right, from which men came running too. Indiscriminate shooting came from all quarters now, even from the higher land. Machine-gunners seemed to be firing into their own men. He-Setsu heard only faintly, his mind wounded. Already a pink-gray compost of dismembered soldiers hid the sand as the rioting crocodiles thrashed about with a hiss and ran, more of them than of men. He saw men actually scampering over low, corrugated backs, then felled like animals caught in foot-traps. He saw arms flung up in V's; a survivor diving into the shallows only to be raised up flailing like a bird; and, worst of all, red filaments of disemboweled men being dragged this way and that, like the strands of a dividing cell. At that point he wondered why he himself had not been attacked and, knowing only that he had not moved, stood on in aghast paralysis even as a new screaming began inland. The crocodiles had moved ahead, but others were coming from the sea to shuffle through the trail of carnage. Advancing on a broad front, he absently remarked. They cannot see me. I am alive. I am not hurt. I have not behaved like an officer.

2

A moment later he became infatuated with his immunity and knew he stood on a reef of fame, velvet-toed, iron-heeled, perdurably elect. An avatar, an idol, a force.

It was fully an hour before the uproar ended. He-Setsu hardly saw one hundred, two hundred, crocodiles pad like roaches back to the sea. Then a burst of gunfire raked the beach, fired by a demented survivor. A round grazed He-Setsu's skull, and he fell among the remnants of his men.

3

I am the biography of Lt. He-Setsu, but I am not his biographer; I am the re-entry, not its explainer. I am the fact, not its idea, and so cannot tell why he survived the crocodile attack, in which a couple of hundred slaughtered 1,160 of the 1,200 troops trapped on the island. History wanted him, no doubt, as did the reference books, and history curbs both minotaurs and crocodiles. After all, the random is forever with us: out of 2,000 radium atoms, one dies each year, no more, no fewer. Yet why, since all 2,000 are identical, do not all of them suffer the same fate at the same time? No one knows. Neither do I, who am the biography behaving at random like Nature.

There is more to come, too, of our Lt. He-Setsu. Left for dead by the remaining few, who survived because no second wave of crocodiles but a relief party from a boat came up the beach, he came to, unthinkingly waded through the maroon slop of the mud, and washed his wound. Then he stumbled inland, as high as he could go, settled behind a machine gun, and viewed the mosaic below of ballooning middles, jagged limbs, and black still heads. The crocodiles had killed way beyond their capacity to eat. Yet they had not returned to their leavings. And, as history knows, they never came back to that island, which they had never visited before. So far as is known.

After an hour's miserable thought, Lt. He-Setsu opened his shirt and began to knife exploratory lines across and down his stomach, just breaking the skin. Soon it resembled a close-up of wickerwork and he still had not made the plunge. If he fainted, he didn't remember the faint's onset. The blood congealed. His head hammered. Nothing broke the even spread of ocean. On he sat, an island upon an island of the dead, grimly reminded of white silk scarves which a Japanese girl would give her sweetheart to make him invulnerable in war. No such scarf had come his way.

On the one hand, he could sit where he was and solve all problems by starving to death. On the other hand, he could commit *seppuku* there and then. But why do either? Turn cannibal instead.

Out of the blue a salvo of shells straddled the island, all but one missing. Shaking dirt off himself, Lt. He-Setsu found he was unhurt. It occurred to him that, if only he found himself in a jungle and not on a bare finger of an island, he could remain there forever, living off the land. Torn between shame and the glory of being exempt, he fingered his sword and then chose: not honor, but deference to fate. Perhaps I am dead already, he mused, wincing at the cuts on his stomach. There is nothing else to do. This is my lot. I am home. Fate will tend me now.

But he was wrong. Only a day later, he was captured by U.S. Marines, mopping up, who found on a knoll only forty feet high a white-haired, blood-caked approximation to a man, impenetrably silent and rigid in a squat. They had to lift him up as he was. During interrogation he was unable to explain to the Nisei sergeant how he had survived; it was as if the interrogator were asking why men bore sperm and women eggs.

Perhaps, he told them all, a destiny awaited him, years hence. A raised eyebrow was the only response he saw. His one prayer was never to meet the other survivors.

4

He never did. It is not known why. I am only his biography, not his exegete. What little help we have consists in his postwar audacity. Driven by some nagging sense of purpose, he took to studying mazes, not as decoration but as replicas of his own life situation. Not as puzzles but as cosmic emblems. For two years he designed and built small mazes in private or public gardens, often doing the digging and planting by himself. Thinking of the crocodiles, as he unrelentingly did, he worked fast. Next, however, he decided to do something serious and, in the dead of winter on Hokkaido, the northern island of Japan, initially with help from astounded peasants who had never been paid so much, built a life-or-death maze with enormous blocks of ice.

Alone, in his parka and airman boots, with a small fire, an ice-saw, and a big thermos of hot *sake*, he stood in the center of his finished maze and dropped the one and only plan into the flames. An hour and a quarter later he strode through the refreezing slush the fire had made and stamped out the embers. Then he drank all the *sake*, stripped off his parka and boots, and bearing the ice-saw before him looked for the way out. Lt. He-Setsu was repossessing his survival and, through it, his chance of death. It is not known what metaphysical yearnings occupied him during his last hours in that ice-warren, but his biography says he froze to death at the kneel, facing south. He no longer had the ice-saw. His stomach was bared and much scarred, as well as glued with recent blood.

No one has gone in; but, when the ice melts in a month or two, his corpse will fit into a legend everybody knows. And his name will come to life again.

# I WILL ARREST THE BIRD
# THAT HAS NO LIGHT

JAMES PURDY

I will arrest the bird that has no light
and hold him tight
his feathers I will straighten
his beak wipe clean
then when the night has closed all eyes
my bird and I will forward fly.

She has gone into silver rooms
and sung four notes
and the birds refuse to answer
from their sapphire perch.

She would never fly in the forest
or sit on tops of great trees
only in dark rooms
her singing can please.

The queen of the night
cries in flight
but the birds in the cage
are silent with rage.

# I EXPLAIN MYSELF

An excerpt from the novel-in-progress *The Midwife*

GEOFFREY RIPS

1

Call me Chuy. Chuy Testimonio-de-Feliz Rodríguez. I am the only known son of my mother, who did not refuse to claim me in the last minutes of her deathbed. And I am not the only son, I will bet you on my soul, of my father, who will wander faceless through the dark rooms of eternity. They also call me son of Old Ofelia. They also call me worse than a cockroach. They also call me third post from the right. They call me anything they want. I don't hear them with their names, always walking in and out of here. What do they know about me? For that matter, what do they know about themselves that I don't see? I see many things as I sit here on the front porch while they walk by me going into the house, refusing to see me as if I were the last doubt they may have about themselves. It's all those shoes and all those pairs of pants with bulging flies that can barely contain what they carry. It's the way they walk up on the front porch already inclined in the angle used for falling into bed. And when they walk out the front door, always the same light breezes are blowing through the new looseness of their pants. I know at least as much about the lower half of them as they think they can tell about me and my infirmities. Some will stop here be-

side me on the way out to ask if my back is feeling better just like
that was the reason they came here in the first place. And I will tell
them, talking to their belts, that no, the diseases of my back will
never be improved. And to do this I have to point my knees toward
the mimosa tree growing on the west side of the house. Then it will
follow, through the painful course of the wandering pilgrimage of
my spine, that my shoulders will be turned as if to face the ap-
proach of someone walking up to the front porch from the street
and my head will then be turned to confront the belt buckle that
has just walked out the front door holding its precious vacuum. It
has been like this for sixty years, the eternal wandering of my spine.
And for the last six years and a half there has also been the palsy,
especially in the shaking of my left hand and the occasional refusal
of my left leg to walk with its brother on the right. It's not so bad,
this shaking. The only thing is when I go to take a piss, sometimes
the palsy starts. That's when my water sprinkles everything except
the target it's supposed to hit in the same way that we often do
something thinking it will lead somewhere and the place it leads is
everywhere except the place we had in mind. That's when I come
out of the bathroom looking like I had just fallen into the sewer
and the women come up to me and say, so Chuy, now you let the
dogs piss on you. And I tell them I do not need anyone, not even
dogs, for that.

But they are good to me, these women. When it is the rainy
weather a new spirit feeds into the twisting of my spine so that I
feel like my backbone is no longer mine but instead it has become
a vine that carries me on its cruel winding through the trellis of my
flesh. When it is rainy weather and my spine goes curling after rain-
drops, the women here take good care of me. Especially Eufamia.
Especially Chabella. Especially Angelita famous for her hands.
They call me to their beds without my asking. And then they take
the oils containing herbs that were prescribed for me long ago and
rub these oils all along the twisted spiral of my body. (I am forced
to say spiral because at these times I can no longer be said to have
a front and a back with which to face and leave the world.) And
sometimes they go on for hours and they say it brings them luck to
rub a body that is so much like the twisted chains of life. And they
forget about their customers and I tell them all the stories that I
know and sometimes I pull stories from the air that I myself did not
know before that moment. And they are good to me, these women.

And sometimes they do me other favors, though I do not require them so much any more. But even a man who spends his life sitting on the front porch of a whorehouse has his desires. And in the old days when business was slow or they were on their day off, they used to invite me up to their beds and in those days it was not uncommon for two or three to have me at one time because the twisting of my back was not without its compensations. It did allow me on occasion to attend to the affections of several women at one time. And in my later years the Midwife would call upon me to go to bed with some of the newer women who were hesitating about some of the things they were asked to do in the course of an evening's work. She knew I could accommodate her. She told them, Chuy is the test for you. He is as far as you will ever need to go. If you have a customer who is more perverse than Chuy, then you do not have to attend to his needs. Do not worry about that. Worse than Chuy and we throw them out. He is the standard of perversion that we use here to measure how far a girl must go. But to defend myself, I must say that what they call my perversions are nothing more than the natural conclusions of my own infirmities. And in these last years I am not called to bed so much. It is mostly just to rub my back or to hear what I know about this place. Except for Angelita, who calls me to her when she sees I have the palsy. She has even gotten me inside her and then tried certain tricks to get the palsy started. And sometimes it comes and sometimes it doesn't. It's hard to say whether it is her tricks that bring it on. She says she has never felt such excitement as when my palsy shakes her from inside. She says it must be what an earthquake feels like to a town. She is very kind. In general, I do not like the palsy. But when I am in Angelita's arms, I will suffer anything.

But I do not want to talk about myself. Who gives a shit about a man who cannot look into the face of the woman he is making love to? A man so twisted that his words of love must be whispered to a wall while he gropes inside a woman. A man who, therefore, has come to look on walls with certain feelings of tenderness and holds a special affection for certain dark corners only a spider could love and certain dampness in the plaster that can make his flesh rise. Who cares about a man like that? Let him cry for mercy to the bricks. Let him tell his story to the baseboards of the closet. Let him grow so old and forgetful that there will be no record of him, not even in his own memory. I know that's what they say. So I won't talk about myself. Besides, why do I want to leave a mark the way the dogs write their names with piss on every fence post and tree? As long as I can keep the space I was born into and carry that space with me through all my days spent walking toward the grave, then I do not ask for any other thing.

Besides, this world is just a whorehouse. That's all. And you walk in and three minutes later you walk out again. And either you have a stain on the inside of your pants or you leave a stain on someone else's bed or you may not have it in you to bring about a stain at all. And that's all life is—the buildup of desires until they are exploded, the way your pants fall off your bones one day in order to tell you that the next time they are zipped up you will be dead and in your coffin. So why should I bother to tell you about myself? It doesn't matter to me anyway. The way life is, it doesn't make a difference. But I'll tell you some things. Not about myself, but about the other people. Not because they make a difference either, but because it helps me get through all the minutes of my life in this world.

So I won't talk about myself. I am the son of a whore who never spoke of the mother before her. You can call me whatever you want. You can call me syphilitic dog. You can call me the one who sleeps with crabs every night of his life. You can call me the clap outright. Call me one who keeps his nose wet. Call me complete remorse. Call me no relief. I don't give a shit. A man who thinks himself worth more than the dried-up scum that is the outpouring of his balls will end up fucking a mirror until his prick falls off. I know this. None of us is worth more than the come that we let go. Let me tell you this: even if a man becomes a great sword swallower, to himself he is still a fool.

2

I'll tell you who I am. I'm the one you've heard about. The one who one day woke up with an acquired taste for the sour stench of the sheets he had been raised in. The one who one day, while hanging on a doorknob listening to the noises a woman makes while working, felt the pilot light turned on in the brick oven of his crotch. The one who went to piss in the presence of the women who used to wipe his ass and found an iron pipe behind his zipper that would not point in the direction he had trained it but instead turned to every corner of the bathroom as the new poles for its compass, the hot balloon that would not deflate even after spilling its contents on his shoes, that would not fold up into its place behind his zipper but instead led him out of the bathroom like a bloodhound bewildered by a scent that whispers to it from every direction, led him out into the hall followed by the tracks of his wet shoes and the coughing of the women, who had started laughing while they were rinsing out their mouths. I am the one who woke up in the middle of the night with his nose buried in the dirty sheets and his body floundering in the puddle of its own fish smell.

I am Chuy The-Gray-Wing-of-Sadness Rodríguez, the one who one night woke up from the dream of childhood with moss growing up the insides of his legs and the understanding that his mother was a whore. I'm the one the story is about, the way it says the boy discovers the two main truths about the world in the same gunshot that begins the dog race to his manhood: the steamy truth about the way his mother had earned their living for all those years he had spent hanging on to doorknobs knowing everything a keyhole could reveal and understanding nothing and the more dangerous truth that now he could be counted among those who come to use her. You know the rest of my story. How the boy steals the gold watch to pawn for his mother's bed. Only it was not a gold watch. It was one of my mother's shiny bracelets, the kind the customers steal all the time anyway to take back to their wives, saying you are the only woman in my life. And I didn't pawn it either. I sold it outright to the hunchback at the market, who sold it again for twice its value. And when I came back with the money later that night in the business hours and walked into the front room as we were not supposed to do at that time and walked up to my mother and put the money on her lap without saying anything, she slapped me across the face and didn't say a word. And no one else in that room said anything either. I remember that. Then she grabbed my hand and took me with her to the upstairs rooms and closed the door behind us and told me, you are right, it is time you learned what it is to be a man like all the rest. So that is who I am, the one who tried to recreate himself in the womb of his own beginnings. Though that would be a crime larger than life itself: to be the one who brought another helpless soul into this world to eat dust for sixty years. But you know the whole story already. I don't need to tell you anything. Let me say this, however. You may not like the way I live my life, but it is not up to us to judge the other people. That is what I think. We have enough trouble just watching over what we do ourselves. So I make judgments on no one. Not on my mother, who always made sure I had clothes on and food to eat. Not on the ones who called her into the darkness of their lives. At least I'm not one of those who, instead of going directly to his mother's bed, walks out the door and comes back ten years later with a diamond ring on every finger and the death certificate of his father that he murdered, who goes to bed with his mother without her knowing who it is and shoots her in the head before she can get up again. You cannot say that of me. I judge nobody. I am who I am. Chuy Harp-Made-of-Roses Rodríguez. But you knew all this about me already. One look at my face tells you everything.

3
I've watched the shitbeetle roll the moon across the sky too many times not to know how long the night is. I tell you that. I am one familiar with the night. Sometimes I make love to it. I whisper, Night, we are the only things that choose to live in darkness; we are the only things that shun a bed. It is like the time the plague of weeping struck. Everyone was touched by it, except for me that is. I came out here on the front porch just to get away from it, to be alone with the night that is itself untouchable. Even the birds did not sing then, except for those that sounded the low notes of despair. Dogs howled all night, and from all the bars you could hear nothing but grown men crying and sad songs played on the juke box. "This is the last day of my life, my love. Other men will lift your black skirts of mourning before I'm in the ground." Men walked into our house holding bandanas to their eyes. And the women were so drunk with tears they could barely work. And from all the rooms I did not hear the soft songs of the women's fingers or their laughter that begins by bubbling in their crotch or the dark voices of the men or their muscled shouting or the women screaming, good yes you're a horse you're a bull you're a warship. None of that. I only heard the dripping faucets of their eyes. The tiny waterfalls that filled up all the bedpans that I used in the mornings to water the geraniums. And these men and women would lie in bed all night crying with each other. And the mildew that sprouted from their tears was curling all the wallpaper with its smell. And I had to cook it out of the mattresses every morning by laying them in the sun. And it was bad for business, the women and men lying there together for so long, the men not able to get it up, the women with-

out the will to make them. And the Midwife through the warped
glass of her own tears saw that something must be done. And the
plague of tears was spreading. All along this block the flowers
closed. Fireflies coasted like dark holes in the air. The ditches on
this side of town slowly filled with tears. The weeping flooded inter-
sections. Nothing moved. Even El Tenampa Bar, where a man
could always go if he wanted to be confronted face-to-face with
the ugly violence of this world, where I go sometimes when I can
take no more of my world of women, where I go to be reminded
that other worlds are worse, even El Tenampa Bar was a rowboat
floating in the lake of its own grief. No one was flashing the switch-
blades that he had for fingers. No one was shooting off the left ear
of the even-numbered people that walked in the door and the right
ear of the odd. No one was drowning in the toilet bowl with a
needle in his gums. In El Tenampa Bar, as in every bar at that time,
the only sound was that of the men refilling their own shot glasses
with their tears. All that anyone could discuss when they could con-
trol their sobbing long enough was the possible cause of the plague.
Some said it was a plague of remorse for the eternal campaign of
killing carried on against the cockroaches of this town. Others said,
and if I were to hold an opinion this opinion would be mine, that it
was the same disease that all the cattle carried with them to the
stockyards, the disease we heard them moaning from as they
walked the wooden gangplanks to their death. And so the plague of
weeping continued. And the Midwife wept with the plague and
with the way it hurt business. As for me, I could not stand to stay
inside with all the weeping. And it was little better outside, but at
least there was the night. And I don't know why it didn't touch me,
this plague. Perhaps because I have never in all my life been known
to shed a tear. Perhaps because I already have a small portion in
me of the cause of such a plague, the way the cowpox can be used
to hold off the smallpox. I don't know for sure, but sometimes I my-
self felt like crying with all the constant misery that left a dew on
the grass in the morning and rose like a mist with the sun. Anyway,
rumors began to spread that there was a cure for all this weeping.
The Midwife heard about it and went to see the old curandero on
Colima Street. She waded through the forest of herbs and flowers
and grasses that grew inside his house to protect him from the
world. His eyes were dry. She saw that right away. She asked him
what to do about the plague of weeping, that she had heard there

was a cure. But he assured her that sometimes a plague of weeping is necessary to clean us of our sins that can clog up all our pores and cause us to grow fat on our delusions. That usually he is opposed to prescribing treatment for a fit of weeping, that tears themselves are a cure. That he could see that this case was special, however, in view of the fact that even certain saints were known to be weeping in their tombs where water could be seen seeping out of the stones. And, furthermore, he recognized the importance of a dry-eyed nature to the business of the Midwife, a business that so often depended on the lasting power of mascara. And, therefore, he prescribed for her the treatment that cannot fail to cure the tears. He recommended a bath in dust that he had imported from the Sonora Desert. The Midwife bought a wagonload and had it delivered to the house. She had me paint the walls with the dust. She had me insert it in our water system. She had all the women bathe in it, and all the men who stepped inside the house also had to submit to this treatment. They did not mind. News of the Sonora dust cure spread in every direction then, and soon the plague of weeping ended, except for minor outbreaks that could be heard on certain corners in the night. Except in certain pockets of despair, the Don Luís Bar for one, the Abandonado Lounge for another, where the juke box only listed sad songs and the people dozed off in the booths, crying in their sleep. And the crying stopped for good, even in the dampest corners, when the dry winds of the summer finally moved into the air and covered everything with the fine silt of the desert that is always hanging overhead.

I could have gone back inside then, when the weeping stopped. But by that time I was accustomed to the front porch as the place to spend my nights with the cicadas and the voices that the silence spills from its pockets at different times and the shitbeetle rolling the moon through the dirt.

4

I am the one who I am. That is all. Chuy Death-Makes-Little-Difference Rodríguez. What more is there to know? Sometimes the people they call me crazy. They say I belong in the house for those who are insane and wandering through themselves. I tell them I already live there. I do that so they will laugh and forget I am here. I do that so they will no longer see me and the twisted angles from which I view the world. I do that so they will leave me to myself. But I also do that because it is not entirely untrue either. And I do not mean that this whorehouse is different from the rest of the world in that regard. I mean this world is an insane asylum where we all go wandering through the madness of our lives. I mean what can you expect? From the moment that we take our mother's milk we are all infected with the syphilitic nature of this world. That is what kills you. It is not the cancer or the old age or someone's bullet. It is the venereal disease of life that claims you in the end. So when they tell me, Chuy you are going crazy, I say, I do not deny it. My madness is proceeding at its proper speed I tell them. The speed of life and death is the proper speed I tell them. And they laugh and walk off saying I am crazy. And I do not deny it. I know who I am.

And the rest of the people who live here almost never think about these things the way they occur to me sitting for so long in the contagion of my own bones. But I think they would agree with me about what I say. I know this is the case with Angelita, whose hands could heal the wound of death itself, because I have discussed it with her, though she laughs all the time that we are talking, all the time that she is working out the barbs from the wire fence of my spine. She laughs but I know that she is listening because she is always listening and she is thinking, too, like the time she told me that life means more to her because it is just out of reach than it would mean if she could hold it in her hand. And I know the Midwife thinks about these things because she is the one who makes sure the thick ball of the world is always sitting in our front room no matter what journeys into heaven and dances into hell are going on in the upstairs rooms. Many times I have seen her sitting surrounded by the business of the night, lost far inside herself. She's told me what she has found herself thinking: what it is to bring life out of the darkness of a woman's womb in her office of a Midwife, what it is like to preside over the configurations that men and women make looking for a way out through the shadows of the rooms of the second floor, what it is like to taste the world forever with the dark lips of a whore.

## 5

But if ever there was someone that I loved in this world of unfulfilled desires, if I have ever felt what the songs on the juke box at Los Buddies speak of when they sing of love, then I have felt that

for Angelita famous for her hands. If ever anyone has caused me
to be someone beside myself, besides Chuy Flesh-Sold-on-Highways
Rodríguez, the one to whom desires as they are known to others
are unknown, if ever anyone has brought me a moment of forget-
fulness of what it is to be an unfortunate galaxy made up of sixty
years of dust, then that person is Angelita of the questioning heart,
Angelita who cannot wear clothes, Angelita who denies the fact
that she had parents, Angelita who lives naked in the upstairs
rooms, who once told me, I feel naked when I am wearing clothes,
I cannot recognize myself that way, I am familiar only with my skin
though maybe it is sad that my own nakedness does not excite me
as I have seen other people excited by the strangeness of their flesh,
but that is of little consequence to me, all I know is that I am my-
self when I wear no clothes and look into a mirror, and when I am
dressed I can see that I am lost inside someone else and anything
can hurt me. Angelita who used to walk through the entire house
with nothing on and go out into the streets at night with people
calling to her from their porches, Angelita go and put some clothes
on, you are too much with us. Who used to meet her customers in
the front room with nothing on until her customers stopped coming
and the Midwife had to tell her that she was not naked the way the
other women were sometimes naked, that the men were frightened
by the way she wore her nakedness, that it made them feel naked
to all that they were hiding in their lives, that the eternal presence
of her flesh was too much for them to bear the way they so often
came there feeling like a pair of khaki breeches masquerading as a
man, like a back that was losing its daily battle with the crates of
lettuce or the highway tar or the cement blocks of an endless wall,
that they came to her to forget all that they are and that they have
never been and then she meets them with her unrelenting flesh
and they are caught without a corner to hide in without a shadow
where they may seek refuge. Angelita who was forced to wear a
satin dress when sitting in the front room and blamed the men for
that, who spends most of her time upstairs naked with the white
walls of her room where the men come knocking calling through
the door, Angelita are you in bed and covered with a sheet I am
coming for you. Angelita who more than the rest of us can look at
herself in the mirror without the gentle shading of regret. Angelita
who can bring the simple grace of her fingers to the difficult stair-
way of my spine, who tells me the trembling of my palsy is the

greatest excitement of her life, this is what life is without clothes on, she whispers in my ear laughing, it is the joining of two bodies by an air hammer from above. Angelita who is forever standing by her window laughing at the boys walking home that way from school to see the revelations of her skin, at the girls walking that way to the store to peek into the future, at the men walking that way going home in order to see her laughing, at the women going to bingo walking that way just to see her. Angelita who says she has no last name. Angelita who was never born. Angelita who has a soul if anybody has one. Angelita who if I am capable of love I love. Angelita walking naked through every song in every juke box that I keep playing over and over night after night that I feel like this.

### 6

Some days I am not myself. Not that I am someone else. But some days I am not myself. On those days I wake up in the morning and sit up in the bed and put my shoes on without the least resistance from my back and walk out of the house and forget entirely who I am. And the dogs I always feel like won't come near me then. They let me walk my own way, realizing I am not the usual person who must suffer in this skin. On those days I walk away from this house, away from this block altogether. I walk the four or five blocks to Los Buddies Lounge and have a beer and sit in the booth thinking that maybe my life is suddenly becoming something that it never was and that my back will no longer be so much what it always has been and that the palsy will not again return to my left side. I think these things completely forgetting who it is I am thinking about. And then sometimes I go and eat a meal with the blind man at the Golden Star and think that now I am a man that people must speak directly to. Some days I fool myself this way. And even going home I think my walking has some of the grace and ease that other people carry. It does not last, this feeling. There is always something that gathers me up and returns me to the person that I am. It might be a wind that shoots into my backbone from around the corner of a building and sews its silver thread through all the painful twisting of my body. Or it might be a dog that recognizes me before I recognize myself and lifts its leg beside my leg and bathes me in the yellow piss of who I am. Some days I am not myself. But those days never last too long. Today I am myself entirely.

You see, these are modern times we live in. They have always been modern times. I tell you this. No matter how fast you are able to move along the unforgiving corridors of life always leading to a blank wall at the end, the world is moving faster. No matter which way you turn to escape your own existence, the world itself has turned that way already and all the other ways there are besides. That is why I live my life. There is nothing else to do. That is the only reason. Everyone claims to have his reasons, but, in truth, that is the only one. Even for those who think they go on living just to defy the dirty joke their own birth has played on them. Even they are fooling themselves. The truth is there is nothing else to do but live and live until you die and that is that. This is what I know. I also know that there is no one who can judge me. I am who I am. Let the world explain itself. That is all. As for me, I am Chuy Vidala-de-la-Vida Rodríguez. Call me one who refuses salvation. Call me sour mud. Call me the irritation of a moment. Call me what you like. Call me the one who is the same one he was the day before and who will always be the same even in his grave, the one to whom the burning fires of hell and the huisache trees of heaven make no difference.

# FIVE POEMS

BREYTEN BREYTENBACH

*Translated and introduced by Denis Hirson*

BREYTEN BREYTENBACH: A SHORT BIOGRAPHY

*Denis Hirson*

Breyten Breytenbach was born of Afrikaner parents on September 16, 1939, in the Wellington district of the Cape Province, South Africa. He studied at the English-speaking, and at that time multi-racial, University of Cape Town, in contrast to the more conserva-tive, Afrikaans-speaking University of Stellenbosch preferred by the Afrikaans elite. Interrupting his studies to travel through Europe, in 1961 he settled in Paris, where he gained recognition as a painter and married Yolande Hoang Lien, a woman of Vietnamese descent.

In 1964, Breytenbach's first collection of poems, *Die Ysterkoei Moet Sweet ("The Iron Cow Must Sweat")*, together with a book of short stories, *Katastrofes ("Catastrophes")*, won him the annual prize awarded by the Afrikaans Press Corporation, Afrikaanse Pers Beperk. He received the honor in Paris: laws prohibiting mixed marriage in South Africa (his wife being classified as "nonwhite") made it impossible for the Breytenbachs to enter the country together.

In 1967, he published a second collection of poems, *Die Huis van die Dowe* (*"The House of the Deaf"*), in homage to Goya's *La Quinta del Sordo*. For this he was awarded the South African Central News Agency prize, as he was also for his third collection, *Kouevuur* (*"Gangrene,"* or literally, "cold fire") brought out in 1969.

Two further collections appeared in 1970: *Oorblyfsels* (*"Remnants"*), and *Lotus*, a series of nine prose-poems to Yolande—yet another Central News Agency prize.

The exploits of a certain Pauus were recorded in prose and published in 1971 under the title *Om te Vlieg* (*"To Fly"*). This was followed in 1972 by a volume of poems called *Skryt* (a neologism suggesting the Afrikaans words for write, defecate, cry, outcry, and conflict) and subtitled "Om 'n sinkende skip blou te verf (*"To paint a sinking ship blue"*); it was awarded the Van der Hoogt prize. *Met Ander Woorde: Vrugte van die Droom van Stilte* (*"In Other Words: Fruits of the Dream of Stillness"*), containing poems drawing for their inspiration on Zen Buddhism,[1] was published in 1973.

By this time, Breytenbach had gained a widespread reputation. In Holland, he read at Poetry International meetings; his work was known in Rome, Brussels, and London, and he had written for UNESCO on apartheid. Yet despite the increasing virulence of Breytenbach's attacks on his country's racial policies in some of his prose and poetry, the South African government had not reacted as repressively as might have been expected. Without a doubt, Breytenbach, together with others in a group of young Afrikaner intellectuals dubbed the "Sestigers" ("People of the Sixties"), was placing in question the fundamental tenets of the regime. This they were doing through discussion, writing, painting, and their life style in general. Nevertheless, the Sestigers represented as well a growth in Afrikaner creativity which that very same regime wished in principle to encourage. As André Brink has pointed out, the writer enjoys a protected position in Afrikaner society: "Throughout the Afrikaner's struggle towards political power writers have been in the forefront; the very movement which first carried Afrikaners to power started as a *language* movement. In this context the poet . . . became the acclaimed and acknowledged legislator of his world; the hero. . . ."[2]

This contradiction explains in part the love-hate relationship between the Sestigers and the Afrikaner community at large and why, for example, in the face of their iconoclasm, so many prizes were showered on them—rather noticeably on Breytenbach. It also explains another attempt to bring Breytenbach back into the fold. In 1972, he and his wife were granted a three-month temporary visa—an event quite exceptional in the South African context. Their visit was sponsored by the Nationalist mass-circulation Sunday newspaper, *Rapport*.

Such official patronage notwithstanding, Breytenbach, before leaving the country, had this to say of the Afrikaners: ". . . we have fallen into the trap of the bastard who attains power. In that portion of our blood that originates in Europe, is the curse of the feeling of superiority. We wanted to legitimize our strength. And to do this, we had to defend our tribal identity . . . and because the defense . . . is made to the *detriment* of our South African brothers, we feel ourselves to be menaced. We have constructed walls. Not cities, remparts. And like all bastards, unsure of their identity, we have begun to promote the concept of *purity:* apartheid."[3]

In the same speech he put it to Afrikaner intellectuals that it is their duty to show that their people are dooming themselves to destruction through isolation. The country, Breytenbach asserted, can only be saved by their black and brown compatriots, while "the survival of the Afrikaner, such as he is defined by those in power and who hold its taboos sacred, cannot be assured unless we refuse our South African in word and in deed."

In August 1975, Breytenbach re-entered his homeland—this time disguised, using a false passport and an assumed name—and lived there in secret for three months. He was arrested, however, in November 1975 and charged with being instrumental in the formation of a white wing of the African National Congress, an organization whose alleged aim was to bring about revolutionary change in South Africa by various means, including armed struggle, under the leadership of the black liberation movement. He pleaded guilty and was sentenced to nine years' imprisonment. His statement from the dock contains, paradoxically, both criticism of South African policies and self-criticism for the methods he sought to employ against the regime. It is unclear to what extent this contradiction can be explained by pressures brought to bear on him at the time.

Although still in jail, Breytenbach's most recent volume of poems, *Voetskrif* (literally *"Footscript"*), appeared in 1976. In spite of the politically subdued nature of some of the poems, they nevertheless remain true to his previous avowal that he "would like to try and write for here, for now . . . the eternal means nothing. It is the temporal which causes pain."

## NOTES

[1] The influences on Breytenbach's work are many and varied. Apart from Zen Buddhism, they include Lorca, French Surrealism, and Neruda, as well as earlier Afrikaans poets. He also draws on the imagery of such painters as Goya and Bosch. André Brink in *Die Poësie van Breyten Breytenbach* (Pretoria: Academia, 1971) comments that "we have in this poetry an electric reconciliation between the highly refined Europe of Paris and the earthdark voice of Africa. . . ."
[2] André Brink, "The Breytenbach file," *The New Review*, April 1976.
[3] In a speech entitled "A view from the outside," given at the University of Cape Town on February 16, 1973, and recorded in a volume of Breytenbach's poetry translated into French: *Feu Froid* (Paris: Christian Bourgois Editeur, 1976).

## BREYTEN PRAYS FOR HIMSELF

There is no need for Pain Lord
We could live well enough without It
A flower has no teeth

It is true we are only fulfilled in death
But let our flesh stay fresh as cabbage
Make us firm as pink fish
Let us tempt each other with butterflies, deep-eyed

Have compassion on our mouths our bowels our brains
Let us always taste the sweetness of the evening sky
Swim in warm seas, sleep with the sun
Ride peacefully on bicycles through bright Sundays

And gradually we will decompose like old ships or trees
But keep Pain far from Me o Lord
That others may bear it
Be taken into custody, Shattered
                    Stoned
                    Suspended
                    Lashed
                    Used
                    Tortured
                    Crucified
                    Cross-examined
                    Placed under house arrest
                    Made to slave their guts out

Banished to obscure islands till the end of their days,
Wasting in damp pits down to slimy green imploring bones,
Worms in their stomachs, heads full of nails
But not *Me*
Never give us Pain or complaint


THE HOLE IN THE SKY

*For our house*

my house stands on high legs
I live in the attic
ho ho
I'm happy here

stoke the fire
blow my flute
when a visitor arrives
he knocks at the door
I just open the window
the sun comes to drink
with a clear tongue
the wine in my glass

and I can't complain;
sometimes the thousand-eyed rain
watches at panes
but can't find a foothold
little tadpoles slipping to the ground

I've chairs and a table
books and lemons
a wife
a bed that folds like muscles around me

in the evening my house is an observatory
this coach pulls up at the eyepiece
and a martian climbs out
come come
I scratch my crotch
let wind into my shoes
no thanks, I'm happy here

stoke the fire
blow the flute
I shake my hands out
doves gallop screaming through the air:
go tell the politicians
and the other idiots
my life is without purpose
a grave, a hole in the sky
but I'm happy here

in the morning my house is a boat
I stand at the prow
my fingers set
to plumb the uncharted coast
limbs of trees in the yard
flashing past the porthole

the tree:
the tree grows red leaves
the leaves eggs
eggs become fists

and molt and die
like old bloodroses,
but my house is sound
that's where I walk around
like a tongue in its mouth
tongues decompose?
the lean man wastes away?
mold covers bones?

ah the earth shudders
the walls show through
the floor splits open: fruit;
my doors are hoarse
the windows gape
my wine turns sour
it snows in the summer
the rain wears glasses
                    small rose hands
but I am happy here


## HOW DROWSY WE WERE WRAPPED IN COOLNESS

How drowsy we were wrapped in coolness on the floor
the smell of turpentine and fire
the canvas white to our empty eyes
the night indifferent
and the moon a smile somewhere outside
out of sight
days pass the windowpanes like seasons
leaves of rain, a face, a cloud, this poem,
I want to leave my print on you
to brand you with the fire
of solitude
no fire sings clear
as the silver ash of your movements
your body filled with sadness
that I want to draw from you

so that you break
like a city, opening
on a bright landscape
filled with pigeons and the fire of trees
and silver crows out of sight in the night
and the moon a mouth that one can ignite
and then I wish that you could laugh
your body filled with bitterness
my porcelain hands on your hips
your breath such a dark pain
a sword at my ear
how often were we here
where only silver shadows are left stirring
alone against you I must deny myself
against you alone I find I have no harbor
in a burning sea


LIKE  SLAKED  LIME

my fire is slaked
I must stand to one side
it's rain that strikes against the roof
and tears the heart from its pulsing sac
the ear withdraws itself dripping with sound

what I could not feel in my heart
I could not resolve in my head
what do I know of my land and its problems
what, when its trees scorch
(how inflamed I would grow)
I don't trust in its future
and know that its past decomposes in stench
each day I remember less of its language
it's rain that strikes against the roof

rain is repentance
and rain is knowledge
and rain is the abhorrent blunting of vowels
and rain is nerve fibers bound; lead sinkers

I know nothing now of mountain or wind
hear too little to harmonize
in the choir
besides the heart has lost its coat and pride
it's rain that strikes against the roof

I neither am nor am not
gentlemen I stand attentive, stripped
for the highest bidder
for whoever can keep the rain from my ears
and show me how cunningly fingers can conjure

it's rain that leans across the sky
I've no more fight, my fire is doused
it's rain that gives life to new leaves
grows more repulsive ears on trees
nails on corpses

all things swell together:
here too there is drought, yet thus
in the stillness of the inner ear
you can be coupled with a self—
your small deaf self listening within the ear


## EXILE, REPRESENTATIVE

*For F.M. and M.K.*

you grow less agile, more compliant
fat squats in your body
like ants in a carcass
one day they consume you;
your eyes burn brighter with solitude

you live as if you'd never die:
you don't exist here
and yet death walks in your body
down through your intestines,
thickens in your wings

the earth caves in behind your eyes
the hills grow still, the emptiness green
your hands and smiles collapse
photographs and pamphlets are pasted
over memories: *experience is a dream*

you learn to beg
and ply the raw contrition of your people
on insatiable bureaucrats,
Officials of World Conscience:
you look through the holes of their hearts; into the mirror

next day you're still awake
your mouth gray with muttering
words swarm
like parasites around your tongue
and make nests in your throat

you're always a fugitive in a crowd
don't smoke, don't drink
your life is a weapon
you go down poisoned with despair
shot like a dog in a dead-end street

sometimes you want to bash the day in
and say: look, my people are on their feet!
here comes the explosion! *Maatla!*
and then you forget the silences of language
ants creep from the cry
from the belching entrails: blind freedom fighters

# HAWAII

SHERRIL JAFFE

Carol Kaufman's hair was blonde, she was tanned, and her pert nose was irresistibly peeling. She was wearing a lei of orchids 'round her neck. Ann watched her in the mirror of the girls' bathroom, where all the girls were gathered before class. This was Ann's twelfth birthday, but Carol Kaufman was the center of attention. She was fresh off the boat from Hawaii. All these girls were kissing up to her. She didn't even notice Ann, the new girl in the mirror. Ann, who had never been to Hawaii.

The bell rang, signaling them into the classroom with the boys. There they stood by their seats and put their hands over their hearts and began the pledge of allegiance, one of the longest speches in the English language. Ann was trying to remember the words when she panicked. Had she been holding her hand over her heart, or had she, by some terrible mistake, been holding her hand over one of her breasts? The heart, she knew from studying Harvey who had studied the circulation of the blood, is not on one side or another, but right in the middle. Yet how could she put her hand right in the middle? She would look like a cripple, which might put her in an unfavorable light. And she couldn't be too careful. This was Beverly Hills. She couldn't afford to take chances. She was the new girl in the class, and she knew that how she appeared to the others in these first few weeks would determine her future position in life.

She had taken the precaution of wearing her new blue Paisley dress. She thought it made her boobs look big.

Such as they were. Ann looked up the row at the girl sitting in the front seat, the most popular girl in the class. Her boobs were enormous. Behind her sat the second most popular girl, with slightly smaller boobs. And behind her sat Carol Kaufman with flashing brown eyes and flowers at her breast. She had been to Hawaii on the *Lurline*. A place for Ann would be fixed in this line sooner or later. "Let it be beside Carol Kaufman," she prayed.

This prayer could be answered. Ann's parents could take her to Hawaii.

They weren't going on the *Lurline* like Carol Kaufman. They were going to fly. It was some sort of business deal Ann's father had gotten. When Ann asked Daddy which airline they were going on he told her it was a White Knuckle Flight.

Ann boarded the plane in Burbank behind a family all already dressed in matching Hawaiian shirts. There *were* no more Hawaiians, the driver who picked them up at the airport in Honolulu explained. All these people were a mix-up, he said. Hawaii was a paradise of brotherly love where everybody intermarried. But if someone had really loved the Hawaiians, Ann thought, there would have been some care taken to make sure that there would still be some around. If there had, in fact, ever been any Hawaiians.

The driver pointed out Waikiki Beach as they drove past it. There must have been some mistake. Ann had thought that the Royal Hawaiian Hotel, where Carol Kaufman had stayed, was on Waikiki Beach. They weren't going to the Royal Hawaiian. Ann hadn't bargained for this.

They were going to a new hotel that was the latest thing. It was bigger than the Royal Hawaiian. It wouldn't fit on Waikiki. It was bigger than one hotel. It was two hotels, plus grass shacks for honeymoons, all of the most modern design. From the window of her room on the eighth floor Ann could see the three swimming pools glimmering and the man-made lagoon far below. She wondered if Carol Kaufman had swum in a lagoon. No one was swimming in this one. Perhaps one didn't really want to swim in lagoons.

A basket of fruit arrived, compliments of the management. It was not everybody who got a basket of fruit compliments of the management. They were special guests here. It wasn't exactly that

Daddy knew the owner—Henry Kaiser, a very great man—but Daddy had been of some service to him. Some little service that for some reason made Henry Kaiser think that they should not only be invited to stay at his hotel as his personal guests at a reduced rate, but that once they had gotten there they should be given special attention. Actually it wasn't Henry Kaiser himself who was making all this possible, but another man, lower down on the totem pole, whom no one has heard of, but who is important enough in his own right, whom Daddy had done the service for. Henry Kaiser didn't know anything about it. He didn't need to. He would never find them in this huge hotel, the Hawaiian Village.

That night they dined under a banyan tree. Ann was listening for the lap of the waves on the beach. "The Shirt family's here," Barbara whispered. Ann turned around to see. They had all changed into fresh identical shirts. These shirts were also of a Hawaiian pattern.

After dinner they took a stroll. The Shirt family was already strolling. They pushed past an idol and went down an arcade where everyone was coming and going past racks of Hawaiian shirts. It wasn't possible for Ann to choose among them or to decide which one Carol Kaufman might have bought because Mother wouldn't consider buying her one.

In the pineapple factory beside the Mormon Temple in the middle of the pineapple field they were giving away samples. Ann had never tasted such delicious canned pineapple. It was only afterward that Barbara told Ann that she had made a pig of herself. She had not wanted Ann to feel bad at the time.

A pig was being lowered into a pit of hot coals and covered with dirt. It was disgusting, and it cost four dollars a person because this luau was going to be quite an experience. This poi they were being offered was very nutritious, but you wouldn't want it, the announcer said, because it tasted like wallpaper paste. "Hey, have you tried the wallpaper paste?" Daddy asked. A brown beach boy in a sarong was squatting by Mother, scooping up poi with his fingers, and sticking them in her mouth. There was a flash. In the picture, Mother looked red. Daddy paid for it.

Down the beach some teen-agers were having a party. Ann could hear their transistor radios.

Ann was being taken for a ride in an outrigger canoe. The beachboys did not invite her to paddle. Even if they did, she knew they would just be humoring her.

Ann was not going to make a pig of herself by asking for something to drink, she was just going to die of thirst. When she got back to the hotel she discovered something in her pants. Neither Mother nor Barbara would look. They told her she was menstruating. She thanked them for the explanation, and went along to the bathroom to figure out this Kotex they had given her. Sitting there on the toilet with the door closed she wondered if she really did have her period, or if it was some mistake.

Lunch was at a lunchroom where Robert Louis Stevenson must have lunched. He had one of his little grass shacks out back. Ann looked up from her fruit cocktail to see the Shirt family eating fruit cocktail at the table next to them.

The light was failing as they stood around in the souvenir shop trying to decide among packets of slides of Hawaiian sunsets. They were leaving for Maui on the morrow.

Maui was not a place that people usually went to, but Daddy assured them that they were lucky to be going there. Mother didn't know why they should want to go there if no one else did. Ann didn't think Carol Kaufman had gone there. She looked across the aisle of the plane at the Shirt family. The Shirt family was the most ordinary family in the world. She took Daddy's hand to let him know what a really great vacation she was having. Daddy closed his fist and extended two fingers. "Want to pet the rabbit?" he asked. There was no way to tell Daddy that she was too old to pet the rabbit. So she petted the rabbit and hated herself for not wanting the Shirt family to see.

The hotel they went to was, as Mother predicted, not very good. But there was no way Daddy could have predicted this when he had made the reservations months ago. It had never been his intention to humiliate or inconvenience his family. Ann was wearing the muu-muu she had bought at Orbach's a few weeks before. No one had to know she wasn't wearing a real Hawaiian muu-muu like the beautiful daughter of the King who must save her father by throwing herself into the volcano that was about to erupt.

The road up the volcano was precipitous, and the driver was driving too fast, but no one dared to ask him to slow down. Then he suddenly pulled off the road. They were not at the top. He opened the door for them, and they got out. The air was surprisingly thin.

"Here is something which you can only see growing high up on the slopes of Haleakala," the driver said, pointing to some stuff growing just beneath the road. "This flower only blooms every hundred years," the driver said. Ann looked at the two silver tufts growing in among the ordinary shrubs. She couldn't tell if they were blooming or not.

The hula dancers, wearing grass skirts, are standing in a line. Tall waving palm trees behind them. Leis of flowers around their necks. Each is holding up a huge letter. In the foreground, in the corner, is the Shirt family father's sleeve. It is blurry, but it is probably of a Hawaiian print. All together the letters spell out ALOHA. The slide show was over. Barbara pushed the light button and they were sitting in the family room. The fan of the machine was still going. The phone was ringing.
"It's Carol Kaufman, for Ann."
She was inviting Ann to sleep over. They had been together all day, sinking into the deep water of Carol Kaufman's pool, stretching out in the sun on the smooth tile. Carol Kaufman lying on the diving board, her chin to the sun.
Indeed, Ann had been with Carol Kaufman almost constantly since she had returned from Hawaii. She had run into her at Ellen's birthday party when her orchid lei was still fresh. Ann had struck up a conversation, saying how boring it was to be back in Beverly Hills after Hawaii. Carol Kaufman had agreed. "Didn't you just love the bathtubs in the Royal Hawaiian?" she had said with a lazy smile. "I never got out of mine," Ann had replied, holding her breath. "Oh, I'm so bored," Carol Kaufman had said. "Come and sleep over tomorrow night."
Now they were in Carol Kaufman's wing of the house. Her parents were asleep far away. Carol Kaufman was running the water in the tub. Then she poured a capful of emerald-green pine-scented oil under the tap. The two girls lay back in the tub. It was the most luxurious sensation in the world.
When the hot water at last ran out, they left the water in the tub, and squatting wrapped in a towel, Carol Kaufman reached behind the set of encyclopedias and pulled out the *True* magazine. Ann was waiting in the big bed. Then Carol Kaufman crawled in with her and started to read her the true story of a girl whose parents were dead, and she had to go and live in the house of her Uncle Jack. Her uncle was very nice to her, and his house was in the middle of a coconut grove, but there was something about her uncle

she didn't like. Her uncle was always asking her to sit on his lap, and she felt embarrassed, because she knew she was too big for it. Her uncle was always trying to kiss her on the mouth and pat her sweet little bottom. She was afraid of her uncle, she couldn't escape him, he was so big, she ran to her room, the door wouldn't lock, she was lying in her bed terrified as she heard his powerful footsteps coming down the hall—"This time, you be the uncle," Carol Kaufman said.

# SELECTIONS FROM THE
# VERSE JOURNALS

DELMORE SCHWARTZ

*Introduced by James Atlas*

*From his undergraduate years at N.Y.U. until his death, Delmore Schwartz (1913–66) applied himself to his art with a singular dedication. In notebooks and ledgers, on stray envelopes, the backs of students' themes, whatever came to hand, he exercised his fluent genius, convinced that writing could be learned by "tuning up" in the manner of a musician. Composition was the medium through which he experienced the world, and whatever he read or overheard or imagined found its way into the copious journals he kept for thirty years. "No day without a page!" he would exhort himself, a requirement he seldom failed to meet. Provisional works entitled "Present Moments," "Idiom," or simply "Exercise" proliferated over the years, all devoted to registering the vicissitudes of mood that swept over him so unpredictably.*

*Among the most remarkable documents of this eager, self-observing sensibility were Schwartz's verse journals of the early 1940s, in which, for pages at a time, he devoted himself to becoming "wholly a typewriter with a definite metre"; in fluent, if impressionistic blank verse, he discoursed on philosophy, the day's events, theories of the universe culled from the* Encyclopedia Britannica—*one of his fa-*

*vorite works—and, above all, literary history.* Where many of his contemporaries had only an academic interest in the lives of great writers, Schwartz identified with them, eager to discover affinities between their lives and his own. *These versified biographies of his literary heroes possess a wealth of anecdotal lore and an intuitive sense of character; he thought of the great geniuses of the past as colleagues, friends, a sort of intimate brotherhood devoted to poetry, which made his portraits seem less reverential than salutatory. In writing about his favorite authors, Schwartz aspired to depict "the experience which makes the man / Arise to art."—J.A.*

O Dostoyevsky! angered and tear-run face!
To be an humbled humble one, to be
Pride and pride downed—is everything:
And lets the writer look straight at himself
As brother, stranger, or strange animal,
And at the wonders of the living world
As if an angel looked for the first time.
The Czar took Dostoyevsky's life in hand
Making him look death in the face,
                                    standing in line,
Waiting with other students to be shot,
The last rites given and the bugle blown,
The dagger broken over the shaved head, the bare
And sanded courtyard still, the sentence read
—And then the pardon, suddenly! surprise
Hardly to be surpassed! (one went insane
And not unnaturally). Then to Siberia
To study this desperate experience,
Married, his wife slept with another man,
Pride and humiliation all the time
(To pry suchwise into the human heart)
Guilt and guilt accepted many times,
Guilt unforgiveable (with a little girl?)
—The cuckold going to another room,
Wondering how he looks, being impotent
—Raskolnikov like Baudelaire appears!
He finds his cleverness is nothing much!

*       *       *

. . . His senses, great palms, stormed by fury,
Keats left for Italy in a sick blaze—
—Now Proust and Rilke, long prepared, begin
The contents of their consciousness to study
For its own sake—outside of daily life,
Proust is a sick room properly,—Rilke alone—
When in the libraries some utter sign
Rises from students standing with a strain
Moved by the language of a dead man's mind
Bringing to kiss—in mind—two loves estranged,
Then, then a downpour of applause, then, then
The Western chorus sings how lucidly!
Have you not seen, as in a glass darkly,
Your face in the car window at night dimly
As if your essence or your ghost? Alas!
—Lawrence with student lore victorious
Returns to the West and his post-war defeat  . . .

                  ❋  ❋  ❋

The literary mind is not mere buzz
It is the only church yet left to us
—Céline, Malraux, Auden, Brecht and Silone,
Thrown up by the period, even as Hitler
(this shows the belle uniqueness of each soul)
Rose to a fame when the Depression came
To new America!  . . .  Farrell, Saroyan, Steinbeck,
This was the best America could do
(Muriel Rukeyser, Clifford Odets
Left far behind as soon as War came near,
Ruined by the New Deal, *lifted* by the Depression)
And Edmund Wilson, who looks just like Hoover,
Went on a tour and in the angels' city,
His wife jumped off the roof; in Moscow, then
He thought he travelled to the Finland Station,
But it was Stamford in Connecticut!
He turned with joy to the poetic verses
Of Elinor Wylie, the wild debutante
—The ten years ended when Trotsky was hit!

Hit in the head, hit in the intellect
By an assassin of the OGPU,
The while he looked upon a manuscript,
Ever the intellectual, ever the critic. . . .

❋   ❋   ❋

Flaubert is pulled two ways; to Mme. Bovary
—Contemptuous of her—and the small bourgeois city
And the deep joy that careful hatred gives
Made fine and full in prose; made black, and white,
Made distant and yet intimate; yet clear.
But in Algeria, the shameless coups
Of Arab girls; of all that is not France
Won by the big bourgeois for railroad trains,
Hotel adulteries and Sunday parks,
The Bourse, the stock coupon, and the dead wall
Built by great property between all men

. . . . Coleridge's heart grew to a monstrous fat
And stretched his pain. And made him seek the soft
And null of opiates. Then he was still
And in the stillness saw how the wide world
Was by the mind created utterly,
Blue or dull grey. And prayed to God!

. . . Howells departs from Boston for New York
At fifty years. The culture city dies,
On the New York, New Haven & Hartford train. . . .

❋   ❋   ❋

When Dickens saw in Christmas all his hope,
When Tolstoy rode upon his green estate
& knew the goodness of the family life,
—Agrarian, manorial, and yet,
Withal, haunted by the Enlightenment,
—Judgement & Praise—until he dragged himself
In the cold night to flight from his old wife;
Sad that the modern Homer died that way
—Detested Shakespeare and feared music's charm

❋   ❋   ❋

Yeats beheld the Players, heard how actual speech
Made to ascend emotion and character,
Tower—and blaze!—before the footlights' white
(The dawn glowed; and not, the sun arose,
Choice follows us, a shadow and a bird)
He heard how actual speech held forth the heart
A dripping bloody thing, tangled and thick,
(A London day, the windows white with mist)
The beating thing which leaped when Hamlet spoke

. . . Wordsworth in Calais knew a pretty girl,
And in tranquillity remembered it,
The Revolution howled on every coast,
And a new day seemed, that a lucid state
Might like a classic temple reign, serene
—But when the rage and terror turned to stone,
He sought in childhood's wood goodness profound,
Turned from the city, Rousseau in the mind,
Harked to the Mariner who talked all night
Of the true world composed by consciousness
And found in Nature the experience
Of innocence. And thought it was the Good.
But turned his face from France. And left the place
Where utmost hope had soared. And left his child.
And left the sources of his poetry
Though now and then,—having taken so much!—
Some light renewed itself—an afterglow!—

Emerson lived in Eden to the end
Or on the better side of Paradise
—Given his point of view, pure eye and heart,
All things were perfect, true and beautiful,
Even the serpent and the tricky body
—Thoreau tried it all out. For just one year.
But took consumption in the end. And died.
(He could not understand Hawthorne's dark works
So full of guilt, unspeakable in depth;
Even as Wordsworth, just about this time,
Was bored to death by Dickens' comedy! . . .)
How deep, how thick, how shocking and how long
Is the experience which makes the man
Arise to Art!

✿   ✿   ✿

. . . Emerson gazes on his soul, serene:
With that serenity, he blesses all
—Pressing the frontier now, the pioneer
Is self-reliant in his solitude
—The Indian scout hears, in the wilderness
Crouched, decrees of silence and of good;
They move through Emerson as fabulous
—His brothers die and his wife dies, too young
In the sick blaze, consumption: yet he exclaims
Life is pure good! goodness consumes all things!

. . . Emily Bronte gazes awestruck, sees
Passion consumes her brother on the moor
. . . The opera consumes Walt Whitman like great crowds,
And like the bigness of the continent
(Baudelaire breaks the mirror, for his face
Enrages him: he cannot look at himself!)
. . . Hardy, old Bones, through my insomnia
At four o'clock when in New England new
Gray grows, your cold and just emotion
Brings calm before my second sleep is soft

        ✿   ✿   ✿

Howells and James go strolling to Fresh Pond,
Discussing Form amid the murmurous trees,
Hardly aware as yet how much has died
In the great war just ended. James is ill,
Nurses himself, learns of shade upon shade
Of sensibility and character,
Carries to Europe old New England's strength,
Renunciation, and brings back with him
A sense the colony, perforce, denied
—Life rich and beautiful beyond belief
When culture has grown old like wine,
                         when great
Nobles go by and works of art are near, near as
The hands and feet! or going down the hall
—with some vulgarity, America's girls
Also know this, and go with him, return
With counts and works of art, quite ruined, alas!

And yet triumphant with Atlantic strength
Because their innocence and goodness ruled
Through paid-for marriage and adultery.
—How international Life grows and dies!
James has to stay in Europe to see clear
The themes that make his mind grow voluble
—He does not know the South has all of that,
The Civil War enacts a gulf for him
—As for how many!—more than Atlantic rides—

         ✿   ✿   ✿

Hugo in Jersey shines like a banal sunset,
Baudelaire slumps in deadly tiredness
And sees his own face in the shining dark
Of Poe's dead face (which like Ophelia floats
Upon the fatal flood): Beauty! he cries,
Murmurs to us of what is after Nature
(Rimbaud abuses flowers because of him!)
And to the chic and pretty lady says,
Look at that rotting carcass picked by flies,
Soon you will look like that, my rose-cheeked dear,
—Sails to Cytherea and sees himself
Hanged like a sack, pecked by birds of remorse

. . . Burns drinks to mount the peaks of song once more,
The more he drinks, more difficult the climbs
This is as dangerous as any brink
The riders of Parnassus leap! Let once the Muse
Dance in a ring, let but one kiss be given,
Let inspiration strike but one small blow
And the pure cold mountain air and height
Of the imagination be known but once
And all may well be lost, all else but gray,
All the quotidian turned then to stone
(Alas, poor Coleridge, old S.T.C.!)

         ✿   ✿   ✿

Emily Dickinson goes to Washington
And falls in love most unexpectedly!
And learns like heroines in Henry James
Renunciation still is left of Christ's
Great castle in the sky and in the heart
—And with what sharpness all Life glows!
Has made the great refusal and gone upstairs
To be an old maid. And to write a poem.
—Emily Dickinson plays like an idle girl
With the beliefs, once fiery to her fathers,
Of blessing and damnation; now to her
Whimsy and mockery; yet they are all,
All that she has who now no longer has
All that her fathers had, the actual
Belief which sets the turning world ablaze

. . . Robinson sees his father kill himself,
Stares at his brother insane, and sees the towns
Where once New England throve like whaling ships
Lose like anemia their strong cold life
—He finds this failure in the universe
And at King Arthur's Court and at Cornwall,
Laureate of defeat in a rooming house,
He plays what solitaire through sleepless nights!

＊　＊　＊

—Dante is stupified by many dead,
Proust delicate pore by pore (O violet light
So strange) of his sick sensibility
Regards. Gide to Morocco goes, pale youth,
There to be "true to himself" (Nietzsche
Echoes in him), and Wilde congratulates himself
With easy empty wit until his *mots*
Become his life. . . .

This chorus cries from noble libraries
Guilt! Shame! Joy! Hope! Light. Light. Light
Over the wide world is our inner wish

—Rilke stares at the Tiger in the zoo until
He feels himself inside the Tiger's will
—He looks from Standpunkt. And writes his Poem.
Then in the end he praises Praise, the Yes
Of the whole being accepting everything
As what it is. Like things. And like the child.
—Dickens draws Fiction's Fame and Interest
From the ale-stained tables of the Christmas week
—And from the Debtor's gaol, he learns of loss
Drawing from evil thus a marvellous wine—

# THE THIRD EYE OF A BODHISATTVA

PETER GLASSGOLD

Poor Murray Rosner. When I saw him last, one thing he said to me was, "I wish I could be with you again, fumbling through the void." Well, you'll understand more about Murray as I go along. Myself, I seem to brush against events with my funnybone, though mostly I dangle hysterically on the edge. Like early in 1965, I was working in a hospital uptown at night as a file clerk: Patients' Accounts, M through R. Sorting receipts being a pretty tedious business, and my first marriage having recently ended in annulment, my thoughts naturally inclined toward women, wealth, and power, with all of which to taunt my former wife. But then the bombing began in Vietnam. I remember thinking: If they try to draft me, I'll leave the country—Canada, Sweden. And for the next hour I was America's conscience in exile . . . Yet waiting out the war abroad was a less fearsome means of protest than prison. If they called me up, I'd go to jail . . . The life of a martyred C.O. turned out to be as boring as a file clerk's. That's when I decided to enlist, go the whole route as a Green Beret, and when I'd done my service in blood, to return with shattered nerves as a witness from the midst of the holocaust . . . Between nine and midnight I managed to foreshadow the chaos of the war years; three prophetic hours was the extent of my most active participation in the peace movement.

Civil rights? That same winter saw Malcolm X's admission re-

ceipt pass through my hands. It was the night following his assassi-
nation, and I was in my usual harem fantasy, when I suddenly
realized what I was about to file. MALCOLM X, it read. And just
above that, crossed out: X, MALCOLM. ("Doris? Come over here,
Doris, for a moment please." "Yes, Mrs. Zimmerman." "Look at this,
Doris. An X. X isn't a name, it's an initial. You got to enter it cor-
rect, otherwise they'll file it under the wrong letter. When when
*when* are you going to learn?") "Hey, look at this!" I shouted. "I got
Malcolm X's ticket!" My co-workers crowded around. "Malcolm X
What?" asked A-through-L. "Yeah," said S-through-Z, "where's this
guy's last name?" I scribbled in "Shabazz" to put an end to the
matter. " 'The buck stops here,' " I announced, "to quote old Harry
S." "Who's Harry Shabazz?"

Sports, revolution—you name it, I've been caught in one or an-
other of its spinoffs. Murray had a theory that "history" was nothing
but the sum total of such absurdities. I remember getting a phone
call from him one morning just a few months before the two little
incidents I've mentioned. "History is dead," he proclaimed, elated.
He read me the headline of that morning's New York *Times*, some-
thing like: JOHNSON STRICKEN WITH HEADCOLD—LADY
BIRD THREATENED.

"Who gives a shit?" I said.

"Exactly. If things stay as dull as this, then we'll know the mil-
lennium is here at last."

Murray had a theory for everything. "So what if I'm wrong?" he'd
explain. "It's all out of my hands anyway." Poor Murray. There
were the little schemes we'd brew together. Open up a decadent
restaurant with class, ur-funk, call it The Seventh Seal—a side of
beef roasting in an open hearth; chained mastiffs, dancing bears;
beer, black bread, mead, mummers . . . Retreat to the wilderness
(to Queens, Staten Island) and surface after forty days, or make it
seven times seven, reborn, purified: the Saviors. . . . Raise cattle
in New Zealand: miniature black angus. "Now at last, an alternative
to holiday turkey." "A chicken in every pot and an ox in every rotis-
serie." For the squeamish: "Meet Baby Angus, the new sensation
in household pets. The kids'll love'm. Mom 'n' Dad'll too." "Watch
bonnie wee Angus trim the lawn." "Fertilize your garden Nature's
way."

So long as anything was possible, the actual seemed tolerable
(another theory). Each breath opened up new waves of infinities;

yet we remained where we were, as we were, viewing the ripples—
I, as I've said, always near frenzy, and Murray with a cynic's calm.
I went from job to job, the less demanding the better, and
hopped in and out of another marriage. "Passive" was what Wife
Two called me or, at the top of her lungs, words to that effect.
When, as always, I agreed, white flecks formed at the down-turned
corners of Tina's mouth, her pale skin became purplish, while she
whaled away at some helpless object: the wall, the sofa, me. Murray
enjoyed her performances. His own wife, Elaine, wasn't half so
lively, he confided.

Tina, however, professed to despise my friend. The last time all
four of us got together, she went so far as to criticize his apprecia-
tive gaze. "Stop! Undressing! Me! With! Your! Eyes!" was how she
put it, pushing her salad bowl into his face. Laughing, Murray
wiped the water cress from his cheek, withdrew a ripe black olive
from his nose, and returned the bowl. " 'With odorous oil,' " he said,
plashing her lightly with the dregs, " 'thy head and hair are sleek.'
A. Persius Flaccus." Tina snarled, she choked. Elaine wept. End of
dinner, end of evening, end of marriage.

Shortly afterward I decided to move to the Coast. "Go," said
Murray, "or stay. What difference does it make, just as long as *she's*
not here?" To which I made the impassioned reply (my head is full
of impassioned replies, however rarely expressed) that in her own
way Tina had been right: I was little talk, no action. Well, the hell
with that now, here it was the nineteen-seventies already, and
pretty soon we'd be in the eighties, then the nineties, then—"

"Then you'll be dead," he said, his voice resonant in my emptied
apartment.

"Right! And while *I'm* alive, I want to *live!*"

He yawned. "You'll be back within a year. Don't write. You'll al-
ways know how to find me."

In San Francisco I expected the earth at any moment to open up
underneath my feet. You needed a car in L.A., I didn't have one.
Went down to San Diego, couldn't land a job. Got food poisoning
in Tijuana. Went back to San Francisco, found work as a hotel night
clerk, and lived for five months in a furnished room situated (I was
sure) over the most capricious fault along the San Andreas rift. And
never a word from Murray, no response to my wretched post cards.
("Just a note to let you know that everything is going great! My job

gives me plenty of time to get around the city and environs. Took in Big Sur the other day. Thinking of backpacking up to Oregon, maybe scaling Mt. Shasta—they say the view is spectacular. Love to you both. XXXX Rollo.") He had said, "Don't write"—I thought it was a challenge. How could I have been so wrong?

When a letter finally came, it was from Elaine, special delivery:

> Dear Rollo:                                           April 10, 1974
>     Murray is missing, he's been gone now for several weeks, simply disappeared. Can you, *can you* help me? Please! I'd go to the police, but it's all so strange, they'd never understand. I'll wire you the air fare myself, just call collect. Please . . .
>                                                        Elaine

I was back in New York the next day.

When I spoke to her over the phone, Elaine had sounded unusually reserved, her words measured. No, nothing had changed, Murray was still gone. No, he hadn't taken anything with him, no clothing, not even a toothbrush. Yes, she *did* feel much calmer now than when she had sent the letter, thank you. Yes, of course she still wanted me to come, though she certainly didn't want to interfere with my new life out there. Why had she waited so long before getting in touch? Pause. This was hardly the time to go into all that, didn't I think.

The contrast between her icy tone and her anxious letter was troubling, but for the time being I put it down to circumstance. She'd be back to her bland self once Murray's vanishing was resolved. By the time I arrived at her door, I'd already mulled over a few possibilities. As Murray said, I'd always know how to find him.

Elaine was sitting on the edge of the far end of the living room sofa, drawing deeply on her cigarette, exhaling with a hiss. (This was new. She hadn't smoked before.) The hem of her dark house dress touched the floor, the lace-trimmed sleeves and neck reached to her wrists and throat; her straw hair, usually loose, was parted along the middle of her scalp and drawn into a fistlike nub at the back. "Well?" she said.

A harsh sound, grinding against my ears. I got up to leave. Next thing Elaine was holding me back, crying. We began again. "Well?" I said.

She was hesitant, shy in fact, and I helped her with soothing little comments. It felt odd to be so manipulative: was this Murray's way? Elaine went through a pack and a half of Marlboros that afternoon (I counted the stubs later). She used the telephone twice: a grocery order to the supermarket and a sick call to Sunshine Corner, the neighborhood preschool where she taught. And she went to the john eleven times, the toilet flushing from the moment she closed the door behind her. Whenever Elaine rushed to the bathroom, I scribbled madly in my pocket memo book, putting down the details, such as I could glean, of her husband's disappearance. "E nrvous smoke alot, piss crazy. Think M gone lat Feb n remem exac must lrn. Wht finibn? No saml prs? Soon see." And so on, with increasing uselessness.

But as you may gather, I was able to learn that Murray had walked out of the apartment one morning toward the end of February. On a Sunday, apparently (this from memory, not from my notes), since he was intending to pick up some bagels, cream cheese, and the *Times,* which isn't done every day of the week. Elaine recalled this because in the special way she reads the paper, she sinks her teeth into her first bagel-half at the precise moment she opens the magazine section, and on the day of the disappearance she had had to go without, suffering, she said, "withdrawal." A glance at my wallet calendar and I narrowed the dates to the 17th and the 24th of February.

Now Murray was a free lance. Under a dozen or more names he wrote Gothic romances and exposés, jungle adventures and sex trash. He researched master's essays and doctoral dissertations. And on occasion he took on long-term editorial projects, such as the one-volume reference books he'd been putting together in the last couple of years for Pontiac Press, down near Canal and Lafayette. It was owned by a man named Drimmer, who distributed by mail order, through men's magazines and comic books, and in regional chainstores.

("Murray," I'd say, "how do you do it?" Holding in one hand *The Pontiac Illustrated Guide to Suburban Shopping Centers. Deluxe Family Edition.* Pointing with the other at *The Pontiac World Traveler's Guide to Saskatchewan by Night.* The book spines cracked when you reached page two, by one hundred twenty-eight whole signatures at a time dropped and scattered; the cardboard casing stuck to the fingers, staining them with lethal dyes; the color illustrations were like mud. "How?" he'd answer. "With pencil to paper. Drimmer doesn't care what's in the books, just as long as he can sell them. So I write whatever I want. Last week Saskatchewan; tomorrow, the world.")

"Drimmer called last week," Elaine said. "He wanted to know how Murray was coming along on the latest job, and when I told him what had happened, he began to yell that if he didn't get the manuscript back, he'd sue."

"I don't think he can do that."

"Well, I brought everything I could to that smelly office of his anyway. Have you ever been there?" I shrugged and half smiled: no. "He's an animal. He had me stand there for twenty minutes while he snorted through the papers and boxes like a pig. And then he began shouting about some missing pictures, twenty-three of them he said, which his wife had taken of Yosemite and Yellowstone and places like that. They weren't with all the other illustrations, they were irreplaceable, and if I didn't find them—"

"He'd sue?"

She nodded. "So I looked all over, again and again. Nothing. After that is when I wrote you."

I told her not to worry about Drimmer. If he couldn't actually prove that the pictures had been here, in her apartment, he'd have no case. In any event, since he'd have to have some kind of blanket insurance, his threats made no sense at all. How much could they be worth, a bunch of snapshots of national parks? I'd see Drimmer tomorrow and straighten the whole thing out.

Elaine blurted "Thank you" in a shrill tone meant to express relief, and we passed, uneasily, to other matters.

"I still don't understand," I said, "what's so 'strange'—that's the word you used, 'strange'?—and why you want my help and not the police's. The longer you wait to tell them, the more suspicious they'll be. Now if I were you—"

"Which you are not. And I don't know what *you* mean by 'suspicious.' Look, Rollo, Murray is . . . was . . . whatever . . . your closest friend. The two of you have always been like this—" Elaine made a pathetically suggestive knot with her fingers. "And . . . and . . . oh I don't know just how to say all this, but Murray did something *terrible* to me, only I don't know exactly what it was he did, and I'm not even sure it has anything to do with his disappearance, so I can't tell anyone except you because it's so *weird*. You see?"

I nodded yes, while thinking no. Elaine meandered on with her story.

Murray had changed, she said—it must have started early in the fall—though not in any way you could easily point out. It was as if everything about him had intensified, and as a result all his good qualities, when magnified, became bad, and the bad, good.

For example?

Take his indifference. Before, it had been a comfort, an anchor; afterward, it was an insult. He wouldn't eat with her, he barely spoke, and wouldn't (she hesitated) sleep with her. Likewise, his joking had turned vicious—well, not so much vicious as mocking; and his theories seemed so removed from reality . . .

I couldn't comment on the intimacies, I said. (Was he seeing someone else?) But the rest sounded pretty much like the old Murray I knew.

"But there's more. Like he'd sit laughing for hours in the dark study, sometimes on the floor or even under the desk. And when I'd ask him what he was doing, or what was so funny, because I could use a good laugh too, he'd answer me in riddles or gibberish."

"Can you remember in particular anything he said?"

"*Mæsh'e gobb'l shæren lish, qyn te qobb'n qosh te qish.* Does that mean something?"

I reviewed my languages (English and Pig Latin) and replied in the negative.

"I didn't think so either. But I haven't told you the worst part yet." Elaine was half off the sofa, clawing at her neck. "A woman," she began, "has her needs and the right to fulfill them."

"Of course."

"And after a few weeks of this . . . this neglect, I felt the time had come to, ah, assert my position. It was late afternoon, like now, on the very day before he walked out. I was sitting just where I am, he was in there." She jerked her head to one side: the study was off the living room. "Well, I went and *dragged* him out from under the desk and um—" Flushing a bright pink, Elaine escaped to the bathroom.

"As I was approaching climax," she resumed, talking through clenched teeth, "Murray made me black out. Then I came to. It was over. After all those weeks. Without feeling a thing. *He* deprived me. I'll never forgive him."

"And the next day he disappeared?"

"Yes. Good riddance."

She'd said Murray had caused her to "black out." How?

I wouldn't believe this, but: with the whisper of a single word, which catapulted her into an eternal haze, and afterward brought her back to the moment. Because now that she thought about it, she remembered being called back by the same sound; her return had been like swimming through oil.

"Well," I said, patting my scrawled-over notebook, "that about wraps things up for now. Where should I sleep? The sofa?"

"You weren't thinking of staying here?"

"Where else? You know I'm broke. Besides, you didn't pay my fare just to leave me on the street; you asked me to find your husband, Murray. Even," I added, "if you never will forgive him. Because it's Drimmer, isn't it, who pushed you into looking for him?" She nodded. "Why?" Bewilderment. She didn't know.

Room, board, and expenses were what I required for my sleuthing. Agreed. Also a seventy-five-dollar advance. Pocketing her check, I said: "I'll be using your sofa for just a few days. I won't need keys. Now, what about dinner?"

I could hear Elaine's even breathing. Two bottles of wine between us, "for old time's sake," and she was, as I'd intended, out cold. (She squeezed my hand before going to bed and sulked good-humoredly when I pulled back. Huskily I ventured, "Some other time." She slammed the door.) Now with my penlight I poked through the apartment. Me, Rollo Schumach: I was doing this. The thin beam a ray gun in my hand.

In Murray's study was a secret place where he kept his stash. Elaine snorted and turned in her sleep as I pealed back the rya rug. I felt the underside of the work table for the stubby magnet clamped there. Squatting, I eased the loose nails from two short planks at my knees. And there beneath the flooring, as it had always been, was Murray's teak strongbox, with its mosaic top, bound in leather straps. Contents: one sandwich Baggie half filled with marijuana seeds; one packet of Bamboo paper; one miniature corncob pipe; two Chiclet-size chunks of hashish; and twenty-three color transparencies of Grand Teton, Glacier Lake, etc. Also, amid the clutter on top of the work table I came across one letter, to Elaine from Tina, postmarked Kingston, New York, and dated March 11— a cheery note to say she was resettled and working and living with "a real man at last." (Well that leaves out Murray, I thought hopefully. But I knew that within a day or so I'd be facing Tina again.) When I replaced the strongbox, it was lighter by a fragment of hashish and the packet of slides.

"I'm Drimmer." A hard, beer-bellied man of middle height. Balding, in his late forties, with bunched black hairs sticking out like tusks from his nostrils, a banded corona between his teeth. He looked me up and down, gripped my hand in greeting, and squeezed until my eyes watered. "Come in," he said. I trailed him into his office, blowing on my aching knuckles.

"Your friend Murray is a first-class A-number-one prick." There was only one chair in the room, behind an expanse of desk, and Drimmer was in it. A plate-glass window afforded a view of boarded-up warehouses; powder blue carpeting spread beneath the feet. The rest of Pontiac Press was all Dickens. "Running off like that, I could ruin the little bastard. He could be thrown in jail. I could sue."

"If he's missing, I don't see how—"

"You don't tell me who I could sue," he slammed down with his palm, "or who I couldn't sue! I got breach of contract!" He waved some papers. "I got theft! I got pain and suffering!" He turned a framed photograph toward me. "My wife, Mildred, may she rest in peace, took those pictures that son of a bitch lost. I could get maybe fifty sixty dollars a piece for them, but you think I give a fuck about the insurance? For only thirteen hundred and eighty bucks? But for Mildred's sake, may she rest in peace, I'd do anything."

"Meaning if they don't show up within a certain time, you'll try and recover."

"None of this 'try' shit. I recover, period. I could buy a bigger headstone for Mildred, maybe landscape the plot. Petunias."

"What's your insurance company?"

A head poked in through the door, then another. "Have a good holiday, Mr. Drimmer." "Nice week end, sir." My watch registered three o'clock.

"Good Friday," Drimmer explained. "I let the slaves off early. You could move your ass out of here too, Sherlock."

Which I did, still holding on to the late lamented Mildred's thirteen-hundred-eighty-dollar slides.

I phoned Elaine from the Port Authority bus terminal to let her know I'd be back late that night, sometime after ten. In that case, she said, I'd have to be satisfied with leftovers for dinner. But how did it go with Drimmer? And what was happening now?

"Drimmer's all bluff," I lied, trying to flex my swollen hand. "Don't worry about him. And don't you worry about me either. Just sit tight"—as if I could stop her—"and I'll be along in a few hours."

On the four-thirty bus to Kingston there was time enough to brood.

Problem: How discover if Elaine herself knows the whereabouts of Murray's stash? Answer: Ask her for some smoke.

Problem: What if she finds the slides gone? Answer: Return them before you ask; take them again later on.

Problem: How confirm collusion between Elaine and Drimmer? Answer: Trap them.

So there I was in Kingston, a little after six-thirty on a warm April evening; ninety-odd miles from New York, looking for Tina? Murray? both? The address on the envelope read Washington Avenue, the two-hundred block, which I found without difficulty: a pleasant street on the outskirts of town, thick with trees and lined with white clapboard houses. Tina proved to be living on the second floor of a two-family frame; an outside stairway around the back led me to her buzzer. "T. Schumach"—odd that she should be using her married name. I felt a certain pride.

"Well, well, little man, what brings you up to this neck of the woods? You can't come in." Tina's first words to me in over a year. "But stay there, I want you to meet somebody." She called out "Hunk!" (or "Stud" or "Monk"—something of that sort), and next moment I found myself nose-to-nipple with the broadest chest I'd ever seen. A great beam slammed repeatedly against my breastbone, Hunk's finger driving me backward to the stair rail. From the clublike bulge that ran to his knee, I gathered that he dressed to the right.

"R-o-l-l-o." My name came forth with the thunder of a bull-roarer. "F-u-c-k o-f-f."

Which I did. Immediately. To the shrill tones of Tina's laughter and Hunk's heavy spasmodic grunts.

Tina and Hunk . . . that was one lead gone. Elaine and Drimmer . . . what of that connection? Back in the bus I was trapped amid a merry band of adolescents bawling out the entire score of *Jesus Christ Superstar*. One youngster of indeterminate sex threw itself onto my lap at the end of an energetic chorus, kissing me full on the mouth. "Love! Bless!" it cried; then hopping up and away, "Christ is risen!"

"F-u-c-k o-f-f," I muttered. I felt the herpes flare on the spot. And then I remembered Murray and our "retreat to the wilderness." Taking out my pocket calendar, I counted back the weeks: precisely seven from Easter to February 24th. I used ecclesiastical calculations, forty week days from Ash Wednesday (February 27th) to Easter. No matter how I reckoned, if Murray in fact disappeared on a Sunday, it had to be February 24th.

I admit to disappointment. Not that we'd ever gone through with any plans. Still, he might've written me. I'd have come back from the Coast. This was something we'd cooked up together. Now there was nothing to do but watch Elaine, while waiting for Murray to surface.

*Love! Bless! Rosner is risen!*

Elaine kept an eye on me all week end long, always looking up from her reading as I passed, peeking out from the kitchen or bedroom whenever she heard my footsteps. Good: if she knew where I was, I could see her too. There was, though, a question of privacy. Saturday afternoon, to get away, I went to the supermarket, the liquor store, the dry cleaner; I also borrowed Elaine's house keys and, without telling her, had them duplicated. I noted too that as I came in the front door, Elaine—wide eyed—was dusting the telephone, nudging the complaining receiver onto the hook ("Hello? Elaine? What's going on?").

The next day, Easter, I offered to pick up bagels and the *Times*, stretching out the errand with a walk down to Riverside Park and a tour of the old neighborhood. I wandered past the brownstone on West Eighty-third where Tina and I had lived for three fitful years. Ownership of the delicatessen had changed; even the familiar blind vendor at the newsstand was gone, replaced by another. On Broadway I was struck in the leg by a go-cart propelled by a maddened infant. A wino called me "brother." And when I returned to Elaine's, she—livid, clutching at her neck as usual—demanded to know where I'd been, why I'd taken so long, or was I in some sort of plot with Murray to drive her out of her mind?

Of course not. How could that be? But isn't it interesting, I mused aloud, how some people always jump to conspiratorial conclusions . . . We ate our bagels in silence over the *Times*.

Later, to break the tension, I asked if she had any grass. A useless gesture. "You know I don't smoke it." Well, what about Murray's stash? She glared at me momentarily. "I'll get it," she said. "You wait right here."

I heard Elaine fumbling with the floorboards behind the study door. I watched through the keyhole while she undid the strong-box: when she saw the packet of slides, she let out not even a rumble of surprise.

In the back pages of Tuesday's paper I spotted this likely filler:

Scarecrow Guru?

STATEN ISLAND, April 15—For two days the backyard of Mrs. Constance Scorsese has been home for an unusual vagabond. Bearded and dressed in skins, the stranger is thought to have made his appearance last Easter Sunday, while Mrs. Scorsese and her teen-age daughters were at mass. Responding to complaints of neighbors, the police have tried unsuccessfully to have the man removed. "There is still such a thing as private property in this country," insisted the widowed mother of two. "I don't know his name yet," the attractive 38-year-old brunette admitted, "but he seems very intelligent and says some very interesting things. Besides, he keeps the girls out of trouble and frightens the birds away from the garden." Asked how she felt about the growing number of teen-agers and hippies who come to view the man and sit at his feet, the lively Mrs. Scorsese replied, "I feel I relate well to the younger generation." Neighbors and local police, though unavailable for comment, are thought to fear another Woodstock.

I scribbled a note for Elaine ("Won't be back till after midnight") and quietly sneaked away. My snare was laid; I'd spring it that evening. Meantime: Murray.

A steady whine rose from the Scorsese house as clusters of young men and women earnestly breathed their prayers ( . . . *mæsh'e gobb'l, mæsh'e gobb'l . . .*"). I picked my way among them, made a path toward the back—and there, Elijah enthroned on the mulch pile, was Murray. A group of girls sat enthralled at the base of the low mound; the savory aroma of baking pastries drifted in the air.

". . . end of the parable of the encyclopedia picture caption writer," Murray was saying. "The illustration for entry 'Meister: *Master,*' being the same but for a blemish as 'Schustik, Meister,' left him no alternative. He must needs *cast out* the engraved likeness keyed for 'Meister: *Master*' and substitute the immaculate profile of the Meister Schustik, with cross-reference in the caption to 'Schustik, Meister'—and thus satisfy all. For if the portrait of the Meister Schustik prove false, would a true Master (Meister) mind? *Rollo!*" He waved away his worshipful audience with the tips of his fingers and patted the spongy ground. "I knew you'd find me. Come, sit at my right hand."

From among the swathes of skins draping his thin frame he brought forth a drawstring pouch. "Have a sacred cookie. They're fresh, chocolate chip with raisins—Mrs. Scorsese made them this morning. As Khadija to Mohammed, so Constance to me."

"Murray, you're already married. What about Elaine?"

"The day she can bake like this, I'll consider taking her on again . . . EAT, BROTHERS AND SISTERS MINE!" he cried. Turning toward the front lawn, I saw two huge platters of cookies being shared around, along with milk ladled out in tiny paper cups. A woman (not unlike Tina in appearance, I observed) was overseeing the operation, clearly the new helpmeet. She looked up at the sound of Murray's voice; he blew her a kiss which, literally, set her quivering. A prolonged sigh ran through the gathering. "Sympathetic vibrations," Murray chuckled.

It was time for explanations.

"Rollo," he began, "you wonder why I laugh. You think if I feed the multitudes with milk and cookies, I'm not serious. You also want to know if I hid Drimmer's wife's slides on purpose, or if I meant to put them with my stash for safekeeping. And you're curious to learn what I did to Elaine and why I left her. Listen and I'll tell you . . ."

It was Yom Kippur, and Murray was reminded of a theory he had of the true pronunciation of God's hidden Name. Elaine was home,

since school was closed; he was in the study—each avoiding the
other, but you could sense the charge, as of ozone, in the air. Earlier
in the day Murray had begun to elaborate, in his usual detailed
way, on the mysteries of the Tetragrammaton. Elaine was more than
disinterested: she was depressed to hear him rave on, and cut him
off with a glum glaze. "So I sat on the study floor all afternoon in a
half-lotus, working the problem out alone. Believe me, Rollo, if
you'd been there with me then, we'd have solved the riddle to-
gether."

The fullest traditional spelling of God's name is with the four
consonantal letters Y-H-V-H, Murray explained, or in Hebrew *yad-
hé-vav-hé*, variously thought to be pronounced Yahweh, Jehovah,
Yahveh. The Jews themselves haven't dared to sound the word
since the third century before Christ, with the single exception of
the reigning high priest of the Temple in Jerusalem (leveled by
Titus in the year 70), who, in the confines of the inner sanctum, on
the holiest day of the year, was permitted to whisper the ineffable.
For the past two thousand years the true Name hasn't been heard,
and God, some say, has been unable to walk the earth.

"It's like Rumpelstiltskin," Murray continued. "Generation after
generation, people have guessed at the Name. With shortenings,
like Yah or Yahu. Or more important, with elongations, such as by
adding the consonant B in the middle as a kind of strengthening.
Still, how do you pronounce it? And if five letters, why not six? If
six, then seven, eight. And so on. One rendering has forty-two let-
ters in all, another seventy-two. But to what purpose? Obviously,"
he said, with an emphatic crunch of a sacred cookie, "none. A cen-
turies-long exercise in graphonemics, crossword-puzzle theology. So
I said to myself: 'Murray, if *you* were high priest, how would *you*
sound the Name?' 'With a low, long-drawn sough,' I answered. 'Like
Om, combined with the Tetragrammaton.'

"And it worked. Because I also had a little gas—here," he prodded
himself in the solar plexus, "which made me hiccup. That did it. I
went over the edge, and I've been there ever since. It gets lonely
sometimes, I'll admit, and every so often I wish I could be with you
again, fumbling through the void, instead of sitting at its center. But
on the other hand: watch . . ."

What looked to be two blood-red apostrophes showed between
his eyes. "The Hebrew letter *yad*, doubled: another shortening of

the Name. You prefer the mark of El Shaddai, God the destroyer, the terror of Isaac? Good, you have it then." The double-*yad* dissipated, reforming into the image of a slightly oblique W. "The letter *shin*," said Murray.

Stigmata then blushed forth on his wrists and feet. Coupling serpents writhed on the underside of each forearm. A large blue eye blinked open above his brows. "The third eye of a bodhisattva."

"And then," he added, "there's my work-in-progress." He pulled back his skins, completely exposing himself to the afternoon sun. A monstrous, varicolored shape circled his narrow torso from neck to hips, pulsing with his every heartbeat. "Peth and Thep, the twined eternal twins, *gemini contorti aeternique,* joined together at the nostrils, lips, and penis. Part of my new cosmology. Notice the bifurcate cord emerging from my own umbilicus—" Murray traced his fingers along the green lines—"leading directly to each of theirs, symbolizing balance and harmony in nature and the ultimate unity of all things."

He looked up, pleased, smiling, a web of happy crow's-feet crinkling around his three eyes, and hoisted the skins over his shoulders. "But back to my story. Weeks went by, I lost interest in my work. Elaine became more and more unapproachable, I spent hour upon hour in the study, meditating on the Name. Before long I realized that knowledge of the One had sensitized me to all others. Everything, Rollo, has a name, the secret at the core of its being. Vocalize it, however softly, and the result is as ineluctable as iron responding to the presence of electromagnetic waves. So if instead of 'Rollo Schumach' I call you—" (I blacked out, momentarily it would seem; coming to, I understood Elaine's "eternal haze" and a return "like swimming through oil")—"the little atomies of your soul jump, as it were, for joy. In time I learned control: levitation, transubstantiation. That took patience, though, and after a few ill-timed scenes with Elaine . . . the reason I left, you see, was to be alone, *all* alone, for a while."

"What's another reason?" I spoke up at last, my voice weak and reedy.

Murray scanned me with his one blue eye. "Rollo," he said, "you're pushing. No one but you would dare. Come, join me! Constance would be thrilled."

I demurred, pleading the business with Drimmer.

"Drimmer! If you want to know the truth, I put a spell on those slides of his. He thinks he's got national parks, but when you look closely at the bushes and foliage—dirty pictures . . . of Mildred."

"Then you hid them on purpose?"

"At first, no. But when he ventured hints about insurance money, I told Elaine, and we decided to give him a little run around. Not that we were going to let him go through with the scheme. Here," he took a scrap of paper from his cookie pouch, "the address and phone of Drimmer's insurance agent. Where are the pictures now?"

"In a locker at Penn Station. I put them there this afternoon."

"Does Elaine know this?"

I shook my head: no. "I think she's got something going with Drimmer."

Murray sighed. Poor Murray. "She'll never forgive me for that little accident. But I was only trying to make it better for her, for me . . . Help her, Rollo. I can't, not even now."

"You want me to go, then?" Yes, he did; though his offer still stood. "But two things before I leave: what does *mæsh'e gobb'l* mean?" Nothing, he smiled, just some childhood nonsense he happened to remember. "And your Eastertide reappearance?" A little joke, said Murray. His third eye winked and faded into his forehead. "Ciao." Ciao.

I dawdled back to Elaine's, making my way there by early evening. The apartment was dark; I roared "*Hello!*" switching on every light in reach, "*anyone home?*" From the bedroom came sounds of scuffling, sheets ripping, bodies falling, feet padding along the floor. A lamp clicked on, and Elaine stood alone by the bed, covering herself with an empty pillowcase. "You're back early," she snapped. "How did you get in?"

Loath to be cowed, I avoided her stare and strode across to the closet. "Where's Drimmer?" I called out. "I'm looking for Drimmer!" I yanked the door open, dislodging paint flakes and plaster from around the frame: before me, in a naked tangle among the clothes and hangers, squashed together like Peth and Thep, were Tina and Hunk. "r-o-l-l-o," one of them managed to moan, "h-e-l-p, w-e-'r-e s-t-u-c-k . . ."

I closed the door and turned to Elaine with distaste. "I said I'm looking for Drimmer. Where is *he?*"

No answer. But someone coughed, and I dashed into the bathroom and flung aside the shower curtain screening the tub. And there squatted Drimmer, hairy and pink, his back up against the white enamel, barking at me like an enraged mandrill threatening attack. I skittered hindward into the bedroom, bumping into Elaine. "Tell him I've got the pictures," I said, "before he bites." "What?" "The slides! The slides! I got 'em!" Elaine turned toward the study, then back to me. "You took them?" I nodded impatiently, hopping from foot to foot. "Jerk."

Just then Drimmer charged, vaulting his bare bulk onto my shoulders. I heard Elaine cry out "Don't!" and then crumpled, winded. Drimmer held my cheek to the carpet with the flat of his hand and drove his knee into my spine. He made crude inquiries as to the whereabouts of his late wife Mildred's slides, while I mumbled weakly and squirmed beneath his weight.

"Can't you see?" Elaine said. "He can't speak. Better let him up."

Drimmer ground down with one final, suffocating crush, then rose growling. "Talk, Sherlock," he said.

With a Word I would have sent a well-placed lightning bolt through his temples; turned him into a May fly; levitated him to the moon. As it was, I could only haul myself wheezing onto the rumpled bed, there to catch my breath. Wrapped now in a long robe, Elaine sat near and angrily lit a cigarette. "Stop stalling, Rollo," she said. "Where are they?" Without taking his eyes from me, Drimmer stood across the room half dressed, shoving his open shirt into his trousers. Low moans came from behind the closet door and a soft scrabbling.

"Well?" This from Elaine. Drimmer was gesturing menacingly with his hands. While I leaned back on the pillows and pulled a locker key from my pants pocket. "Penn Station," I declared. And as both of them lunged forward, I airily flung the key through the open window. There was silence in the room when, moments later, it landed with a faint ping in the alleyway six flights below.

Howling, Drimmer sprang to the casement and searched the darkness. "Mildred! I'm coming!" Still barefoot and unbuttoned he fled to the living room and out the front door.

"Pretty cute," Elaine snapped.

"I know. It was the wrong key. The right one's in the mail. To Drimmer's insurance agent. With a note of explanation. Wasn't that something like Murray's original plan?" She seemed abashed. "Thir-

teen hundred and eighty bucks split two ways? As if Drimmer
would ever fork up your share anyway. He bullied you into trying
to find Murray: why, if not to strengthen his claim? At least you
were bright enough not to tell him where the pictures were. Or
maybe you just hadn't gotten around to that yet."

Hanging her head, Elaine trailed after me as I set about packing
my bags. "You can't go," she whined—with what mixed feelings?
"What about Murray?"

"I've found him," I said, "but he's not coming back." It was with
difficulty that I explained, with oblique references to drugs and
occultism (Elaine mused: "I thought so"), and none whatsoever to
Murray's unhappy twins, his bold third eye, or the widow Scorsese.
"He asked me to help you," I concluded, "he said he couldn't any
more."

Elaine seemed moved. She touched my arm. "Then why are you
leaving?"

Ash cans rattled hollowly in the alley. "Because of Drimmer," I
answered. Tina and Hunk moved ponderously in the closet. "Be-
cause of them."

"I'll throw them all out, never see any of them again."

"And because of you," I added, shutting my bags. "But I'll be
back in a few days, because of Murray."

Easy enough to lie. It has been harder to decide my next moves.
Join Murray? Hitch back to the Coast? Or head to New Zealand, for
that matter, to breed miniature black angus. Such an infinitude of
choices. A mass of names.

# LOVE POEM

RÜDIGER KREMER

*Translated from the German by Breon Mitchell*

it was a mistake even
to give you a name
baltic madame
and
one doesn't write
love poems
in november

i should have preserved you
like an antique garnet ornament
of burnished gold on silver
in cases of velvet
or
better yet
you might have survived
the hard times
in your great-grandmother's
portrait

in a white country house
with balconies towers balustrades
you stand
behind the tall windows
and look
through rain-misted panes
upon empty flower beds
and bare tree-lined lanes
where on these november afternoons
piles of leaves are burning
and see
without having really noticed
that the rain
is already turning
to snow

are sadder even
than all the ballads and all the nocturnes
(your fingers too numb for the études)
freezing
in your thin dress
of lavender-scented silk
ah lavender
that is not the season for memories
of southern wanderings
wrapped
in a jacket of smokeblue wool
you fear
winter and sonatas
monograms
sewn white in white linen
letters
from old women and young men
russian cousins
with shorn heads and dark eyes
in which at twenty
a longing for death already smolders

a swarm of black birds
swirls
over your house

i would have found you in novels
and in films
anemic
consumptive and blonde
a child
with little pierced ears
how gladly i would have helped you
onto your brown pony
demoiselle
and dreamed of your little boots
of the many tiny buttons

# MY FATHER WAS A RIVER

COLEMAN DOWELL

They called me a good child. It made me feel even more set apart, a sort of social leper, for this was the great period of rebellion when youth roamed the streets, rode through the countryside like gathered lightning, and the eternal rule of thumb was that it be affixed permanently to the nose. My parents' indictment had another effect upon me. It caused me to husband my dark energies, out of a sense of loyalty, until I became a walking dynamo. Nothing, through those long formative years, was spent, and there were times when the buoyancy of my reserves made me feel that I might fly straight up into the air and hover above the treetops, looking down and laughing to see their faces. This was the most innocent of my fancies. Another was that I should suddenly, when the family had assembled—aunts, uncles, cousins, grandparents—fly into an orgy of rage and kick tables, legs, faces, until all became splinters. This impulse would disappear when I lay before my tall window, washed in the odor of midnight and summer roses. Then I would simply grow and become grass and willow trees, hovering protectively over my mother's grave, watered by my father's dear tears.

My mother was a light woman, quick and evanescent. When she entered a room she had already left it. Her beauty was contained to the point that little of it showed.

When my father entered a room it became too crowded, for there seemed to be too many of him. He extended himself so that he sat in every chair and filled each corner. My father was feral; if he filled a room, he *became* the forest. My father was a river, a fox, a mountain lion.

In a time when large families were fashionable, my parents were considered odd to have only one child, and perhaps they were pitied. But I knew things that I could have told; things gleaned as I prowled the house listening to conversations and other sounds. I discovered in my parents a sort of desperate passion that would bring my father hurriedly home from his supervision of the fields at all hours of the day, and kept the house murmurous and restless through nights when child and servants were thought to be sleeping. If other eyes had been as watchful as mine they would have seen glances and touches exchanged in the midst of large gatherings, and departing guests detained past a seemly hour for the same reason that I forced myself to eat slowly through a dish I did not like, but with my eye cocked voluptuously on the dessert that I loved and knew would be the better for the waiting.

It was my mother whom I watched mostly, for her reactions. I came to know her responses to my father's touch and glance until her gestures and movements became my own. When I was alone with her I would stroke her arms and the hands that I had seen tremble for him. When I was small this did not seem unnatural to her; it pleased her and she would laugh and muss my hair, not knowing that it was myself that I caressed. But later, toward the end, she would pull sharply away and her eyes would follow me with their haunted look as I jauntily left the room at her command, turning always in the doorway to salute her in filial obedience.

But when I was younger they called me a good child. Because they trusted me, I was free. Our doors were never locked. I came and went, harboring myself, and for one whole year I did not sleep at night.

*The River*

I knew many things about my father that no one else knew. An ordinary person with ordinary vision can turn his powers of concentration upon a single object and eventually time will reveal to him each mystery, flaw, and virtue of that object. A stone or a leaf, given the outside force of absolute concentration and the added dimension of time, will unlock itself and lay bare its secret. But my

vast reserves of energy, coupled with my singleness of mind, gave
me an insight that verged on the supernatural; my imagination was
a circle and my father was its nucleus.

I loitered on the edge of my twelfth summer, a dark child filled
with heavy secrets, when the first in a chain of revelations presented
itself to me. It was my favorite hour, midnight—that perfect hour
when struggling day has been completely devoured, its tail disap-
peared down the throat of night. I lay before my window listening
to the tides of sound. I heard the river and I heard my father, both
advancing and retreating, both responding to the syzygal arrange-
ment of sun, moon, and earth, each helpless and triumphant before
nature. Suddenly the sounds became one. As with all true revelation
the answer was simply there. I had been resting naked; I rose and
put on the garment nearest to hand and in that gesture, which was
a decision, I pledged myself to the quest.

Through the summer I clung to the river banks until each angle
knew me by heart. At the beginning, my nocturnal footsteps would
send up showers of nightbirds like sparks from a fire, but eventu-
ally they came to sit quietly and let me walk among them. I
watched snakes moving from darkness to darkness through the
moonlight, their dizzying motion like shored ripples from the river.
Gradually the unnatural quiet brought about by my invasion be-
came filled with the normal sounds of a summer night: chirping,
shrilling, mourning birds; sharp yelp and mutter of foxes; thump
and chatter of beaver; and other sounds of beasts unnamed by man
who inherit the earth when the sun falls. Over, above it all, was the
song the river sang. It was a love song that said *come to me,* and
nature responded. Birds hovered and dipped swooming; beavers
flopped sensuously as they tried to dam up the river's love for them-
selves alone, chattering indignantly when love slipped through their
obstructions and went running lightly the length of the land calling
come to me. I felt its lure, I felt it, but I played flirt, running along
the shores calling *come to me,* mockingly, *come to me.*

And the night came when I saw the waters advancing to my call.
I was not prepared and fell back and heard the river laugh. The
night was filled with the deriding sounds of laughter. Scratch a chal-
lenger, they implied, and you will find a coward; scratch a flirt and
you will find a fool. I took off my clothes and in front of all nature
went into the arms of the river. Nature, voyeur, avidly watched as
I struggled in the grasp of the river crying, catching at roots and
branches—"No, father; oh, father—don't."

For a week afterward I kept away, angry and ashamed. But like most lovers' quarrels this one too ended and I was back, cajoling, mocking, wary. I wooed and was wooed, but at a distance, by night. It pleased me, when noon shadows lay on the river, to sit by my father as he fished, dabbling my feet and crooning innocent songs, watching him secretly, feeling his knowing that some secret area of himself had been touched but little dreaming . . . And so I passed the summer.

When frost came the river's ardor chilled. Spurned and spurning, I looked for new diversion. I found it soon enough.

## The Fox

One night when the lateness of the hour and the increasing intensity of my parents' glances told me they would soon go up to bed, a great uproar came from the direction of the tenements where our poultry lived in constant bickering, complaints, and uprisings. My father shouted for the servants but they were long asleep, and if they woke at the sound, merely wrapped themselves more securely in their armor of indolence that my parents had indulgently encouraged to grow, layer by layer, through the years. Resigned, my father lit a lantern and together we left the house. As we neared the source of the trouble my father stopped. I saw on his face a look of passionate amusement and satisfaction as he gazed at the fox who was emerging from the poultry house, a hen dangling from each corner of his mouth. The fox and my father wore the same expression. They were one. The revelation came as simply as the first. My father, because of the sound I made, gave me a long look then turned, saying "Too late," and walked back to the house.

It was that night that I began this record of my days and nights, suspecting mortality.

The following evening I sat shivering on the roof of the summer house glaring at the moon for its coldness when I saw the fox moving past me. I turned my head slowly so that its motion might be mistaken for the turning of a star but I was caught out. The fox and I exchanged a look of comprehension. He read my disdain for hens and I his desire, which, considering our position, amounted to the same thing. I longed to become an accomplice, a procurer, a pimp, whose reward would be one bloodstained feather. I felt the same excitement I had known in the river's embrace and recognized the need for control. I let him pass but stayed in suspension of breath and thought until he returned with his victim, leaving a trail of blood on the rimy grass. Again he paused and looked at me and his eyes were filled with mockery and a kind of love.

For many nights I let him pass and the moon waned. He came to accept me there, to look for me. I encouraged his trust and praised him with my silence. Gradually I led him to know that without me he was in danger; that our ritual greeting equaled safety. When the mockery had gone from his eyes and only love remained, when his dependence upon me was entire, I knew the time had come but still I waited, in the manner of my parents and their detained guests: only one lesson in passion is needed by the willing pupil.

The time came when I could bear the burning no longer. An hour earlier than usual, I took a lantern and went into the poultry house. In a quiet frenzy I evaluated, chose, discarded, considered, rejected. I was a connoisseur in the slave market as I deliberated over each point of beauty and desirability. I left no feather unturned and when at last I chose I believed I could feel even the victim's approval. I then closed every possible means of access to the buildings, sealing in the hens like Oriental queens. Darkening the lantern, I settled down outside the tomb to wait.

I imagined him pausing before the summer house, smiling upward; saw the confidence change to bewilderment, the love to doubt, then fear. I saw him tremble on the brink of turning back, tensing as each gust of wind sent a leaf down with death rattle in its fall. I felt his heart flutter and hurt with betrayal, then the tide of his rising anger and arrogance. With him I experienced the desperate decision to brazen it out, then the step backward, the agonizing remembrance of familial duty and the reckless plunge forward on a crest of maleness.

Because we knew these emotions together, when we were finally face to face it was in a kind of love-death. The night eddied around us; we were the center of the whirlpool; the walls were high and sheer and the roar deafening. I watched the pulsing of his heart under the red-gold shield of his chest and my own heart swelled to bursting as I held out to him my gift. I was breathless with his love as the cock crew and a ring of fire swept the sky.

Farewells are a promise of forever and by arresting love at its peak we remain on that high plateau where the climate is constant and the winds invariable.

The winter, like a huge snake, wrapped its gray coils about the countryside. Wild youth still roved and marauded or so I was told at family gatherings. They called me a good child and I lowered my eyes to hide the flickerings of my splinter impulse. The hearth crackled with my father's heat and the house toasted in his embrace. Skittish aunts basked under his warmth and dreamed of assault. A slight snow flurry was enough to make them stay over for days; at night they would leave the doors of their bedrooms ajar and scamper about the halls like mice in their unlovely shifts at the sound of his step on the stair.

He looked at me and by smiling in a way I had practiced in front of the glass I caused something dark to appear in his face. It came first to the edges of his mouth; by concentration I forced it into his eyes, so near the brain. I would hide from him and stay away for so long that he would come to look for me, forgetting my mother's hand on his arm. I felt his restlessness grow and the puzzled lines that came to mark his forehead were as sharp as music to me. One night when I had been playing the fool to the accompaniment of my aunts' laughter, I turned to my mother for the approval of her smile and found instead the chilly watchful eyes of a stranger.

I was standing on a low stool, for in my game I was Icarus preparing to flee the labyrinth at his father's command. The devil caught hold of me at my mother's cold look and before I flew I improvised a speech to my father, playing upon the words "son" and "sun," giving to the labyrinth a dark meaning as I exhorted my father to free himself from bondage to those passageways and fly with me.

When I flew, I deliberately fell and cried with pain. My father ran to help me up. I gave him, for the smallest moment, the look of the fox—knowing, amused—and returned the pressure of his arms as I said without emphasis, "No need to bother, I am nearly grown." When I turned from him my mother was leaving the room, a spot of color high on each cheek. She looked as if she was overheated by the fire.

Through the rest of the winter nights I crept crunchily around the world and once I saw the mountain lion. It was the same lion, I was certain, that had thrown the countryside into a state of terror a few years back, causing parents to lock their children in the houses after nightfall and themselves keeping close to home and light. As all things came to my father's doorstep, so had the lion. Looking at the beast I remembered the way it had come about:

I was a small child in the reign of terror, plump and brown, a juicy morsel to tempt a hungry lion, but in conformity with my parents' enlightened ideas I was as free as ever to come and go. Occasionally in my travels I would be found and carried home, kicking and biting, by some irate community-minded father, and delivered to my parents, and I would see the accusing eyes of my deliverer met by the barely polite indifference of my father and mother. As children are easily frightened by adults, I should have been frightened by the fear in my deliverers, but I only resented their intrusion as my parents did, and I grew adept at eluding them. It became a game to show myself at a distance and when the man approached, scolding, to disappear, leaving my spluttering, cursing, would-be savior to thresh the underbrush while I laughed in my burrow or tree.

One day at dusk I stood with my father in the courtyard of our house, watching the stars appear and dutifully naming them. The mountain lion walked through the gateway and stood considering me. I did, then, feel a quiver of fear and turned quickly to my father but he did not pick me up or shield me with his body; he did not move from his stance of casual contemplation. I looked at his face, thinking perhaps he had not yet seen the lion. . . .

Now, recalling the face he wore as he returned the lion's gaze, I felt the familiar shiver of recognition. It was enough for the time being. I was tired; I followed my sun-filled tracks home and slept all day in the granary on sacks of summer-holding wheat.

The rest of that winter I confined my night journeys to a small radius. By day I read the classics, for I wanted to be well rounded and worthy. I gave my body more care than ever before, polishing my skin with pumice. During those pleasurable exercises I stumbled onto the fact that imperfection can be smoothed away as gentle erosion smoothes away prominences from the land. No part of me escaped rigorous discipline; my hair was brushed until it glittered, my fingernails were made to reflect objects, my ears glowed, and each delicate muscle of my body gained and held its proper importance to overall balance. As I transformed myself I told myself the reason: I was preparing for the greatest adventure of all, the adventure of facing Death, bare and pure. As a great gladiator honored with a magnificent adversary would prepare himself with purging and prayer, so I went about my task, with one difference: I observed the ritual purging, but omitted the prayer. My task was secular—a better word than profane, Mother, though you may not agree.

The change in me did not go unremarked. My maternal grandmother, who romanticized each detail of daily life into little pastel-colored shapes like candied violets, declared that I was the model for all children, a paragon of all known and a few invented virtues. She pronounced me beautiful and her heart fluttered, she said, for the helpless state of the object of my romantic intention. She appealed to my mother for corroboration of her statements.

If I had had any pity in me I would have felt it then at the changes in my mother. She had always been a tremulous woman, a reflection rather than the light itself, but now the reflection was beset with shadows and the shadows threatened to obscure the thin ray. There was something in her of a firefly in a dark glass, the tiny glow, as air is sucked away, growing fainter and fainter, the dark areas of the glass seeming to loom larger by contrast. I saw her thin fingers tremble as they smoothed the material of her needlework. She had not even the strength of her coldness now, but still her look contained no entreaty. I had thought her weak and slow but she was neither in its true sense. She alone had guessed what until then only I myself knew and our shared knowledge drew me to her. I stroked her hair and long pale hands. I kissed her cheek and called her pet names of early childhood while she sat helpless under my grandmother's benevolent eye, her skin lumped with revulsion.

*The Mountain Lion*

When the thaws began green things again fingered up through the soil and out from their polished caskets of wood buds pushed their lazarus heads. At dinner one night I sang to my zither and had the satisfaction of seeing tears in my father's eyes. Pushing my advantage, I made the strings murmur like a river and jump like trout. My father turned a full gaze on me and I blanched. I pretended that faulty tuning of the instrument was responsible for the sounds and I busied myself with the pegs until he partly withdrew his suspicion. But that night when the house slept I sought out the lair of the mountain lion.

My father had taught me about degrees of beauty, from the planets through Euclid and Pythagoras to Homer to the fox; but here was Beauty.

Tawny would be his color if tawny is also the color of autumn's essence and the heart of fire. If one drop distilled from a vineyard's perfect year should be tawny, then let tawny suffice for him. But to try to describe the eyes, the motion—how does one describe a shape outside geometry's rules? If not recognizable as a shape might it not as well communicate itself as an odor, or Death? I felt his glance and if I say I burned and froze it is because there is no word for their combination. If his breath sated and starved me, what else can I say except sated and starved? I died and was born, dreamed and woke, fell and flew. Dawn came, and empty air.

The pattern became fixed. The trees grew fuller, the grass taller, the dawns earlier. Then one night he did not come. Nor the next. On the third night of futile watch I knew he would not come again and I knew why: I guessed his secret, which was that he had guessed mine.

The following night I slept in my bed for the first time in a year.

That spring procreation covered the land. All things seemed determined that their species should overrun the world. My thirteen cats filled the nights with the caterwauling of their love agonies. From the stables, whinnyings, lowings, and bleatings kept the air in turmoil. The aviaries, the poultry houses, the sties pulsed with reproduction. Under the persuasion of nocturnal torrents and daily deluges of sun the wild vegetation threatened to encompass and engulf all cultivation. Modest and timid vines became boa constrictors, thorny shrubs put forth daggers, and the little yellow lions of the grass became full-fledged kings of the jungle. Flowers poured out so much perfume that the garden was a charnel house of stench. In the orchards fruits grew so quickly ripe that each globe dangled a starry bloom from its tip. In the meadows the breeding ponds resembled fountains, so constant was the leaping of silvery bodies into the sunlight.

And my mother's youngest sister, half her age and painfully delicate, sent a message that she was shortly to be brought to childbed and was in terror for the survival of body and soul together. Would my mother come to her?

As my mother went about her preparations she seemed to be imprinting each detail of the house in permanent image on her brain. When I saw her gazing intently at some object she especially favored I would insinuate myself between them; her efforts to keep from seeing me gave to her eyes a look of permanent unfocus, like a madwoman's.

On the day she left we gathered in the courtyard to say good-by. She stood surrounded by servants laden like pack animals. She turned to my father in the pale sunlight and said something I could never forget were I given a lifetime in which to try. She held up her hand at his protesting for the hundredth time her going and said: "Don't protest too much, my dearest, or I might stay. And oh, I don't wish to be spiteful." Then she turned without a word or glance at me and a small wind lifted the end of her long scarf high into the air so that for a beautiful moment she seemed, with her characteristically tilted head, to be hanging on a thread of scarlet, suspended from the wind. The procession moved from the courtyard and each blowing flower of spring sent one blossom each after them and veiled them in a shower of petals.

## Chaconne

Alone. Silence is a pool and the weight of unspoken things sends ripples spiraling upward and upward, limpid O's that are both question and answer, mouths shaped to surprise and assent. Long spears of sun penetrate the pool but stop short of the final illumination of whatever lurks at the bottom, illusively flickering as a thought flickers unformed in the brain's wellsprings behind the eyes. A stair creaks, shifting weight, and the sound is anticipatory of assault, a bracing sound that stirs the caryatids on the newels, causing them to shift the entablature that is their cross and reason for being. The movement extends upward through the house to architrave which, shifting, causes movement in the figures of the frieze, whose pavanne resettles the cornice. The energy rises like smoke through chamber above chamber and dissipates on the wind, which enters the regions beneath the house where the statement originally began.

Everywhere, inside and out, the movement is restated as an upward sifting of thought. The glass of the day is no longer cloudy; each image is reflected as undistorted image. Truth, shedding its dark garments, showing its primeval bones unadorned, walks through the garden. The unsmiling face of Truth is a distant cry from a child's learning. Truth is only part of the equation pointing by parallel lines to a sum of frozenness—a lump of ice without the powerful grace of refraction. The eye, having gazed on Truth, turns forever inward, blind to the world, the shriven pupil staring at the flower of evil that stands to the right of the heart in the precise center of the Self.

Is this the soul you spoke of, Mother? Is this the result of the seed you planted in me early, conscientious gardener that you were, abiding by an Almanac of Faith that led you, in the proper phase of the moon, to teach me to say—without understanding, like an articulate plant—"Spes mea Christus"? Is it my fault alone that the seeds sprouted wild and black branches like a growth from some swamp planet? Weren't you able to see, by the games I played, that the harvest would be alien? But what could you know of the dangerous games of a child in the night when your own elaborate night kept you occupied in a long search for variations on a theme!

But wait—no recriminations, I swear. Only pause, you and your caravan, on whatever plain you find yourselves. Never mind the night; you are safe, wrapped securely about with loyal protectors and noble intent. Stop, I beg you, and think of me, for I am left alone in a house with a river, and a fox, and a mountain lion.

See me now, for this moment, and try to understand what I tell you: Here is my room and I am here by the window. There are shadows behind me. I remember once, in winter, I boasted that I could make spring appear by releasing my stores of energy. Are these shadows behind me deeper than winter? They must be for I cannot budge them. Outside the window are roses—black, drained of the sun. Black grass, too, and trees—a world of silhouettes. On your plain, rosy with afterglow, it may be hard for you to look into the gloom of mine but I ask you to try.

See me, then, as someone you knew, poised on the edge of a world you suspected; a world, however strange, that was made at least bearable by your inability to visualize true evil. And this is the crux: I find myself where I am at this moment by the same inability; I will let you decide whether it is virtue or fault.

I was only playing a game! All children's games are composed on formulae that are dangerous: pentacles, bits of glass to catch the eye of Beelzebub, Runic rhymes; the games you played as a girl could have led you as easily to this precipice but you were probably saved by an unasking innocence. But suppose you had asked—and looking, found a shape, squat and dark, in the center of your magic circle? Would you not have called to your mother then, perhaps on her way to visit an ailing relative, "Wait, stop, understand"?

The house trembles with sounds. If only I were not able to identify them. There is water, stilly and deep, but we are in a state of truce and its gentle lapping could comfort me. And that sharp bark, too, is somehow playful and the appetite that it announces could be assuaged by a hen or a net of birds. We have had our day—the river, the fox, and I—of mutual benefits on a high plateau.

There is another sound. It is of restlessness, of constant movement; not gentle as the river nor peevish as the fox. It is purposeful and sharp in intent as the clacking of claws on the floor. It is the sound of a Titan hungry after aeons of sleep, all appetites become finally one.

Wood splinters, something falls, matter gives under force. A Titan, after so long a sleep, would not understand the function of walls and doors, would he? He would simply crash through.

And a child. What is a child to an aroused Titan?

What is a child?

# EIGHT DRAWINGS

HERMANN TALVIK

*Introduced by Aleksis Rannit*

HERMANN TALVIK, AN ESTONIAN VISIONARY

*Aleksis Rannit*

1

From the eighteenth century, when drawing achieved considerable freedom under the leadership of the Italians and French, until the present, when artists of many countries produce drawings with various techniques, this craft has gained little independence as a sovereign art. Even the materially monumental drawings of today (how miserably small they often appear compared to the tiny sketches of Rembrandt and Goya!), when they are composed in black and white only, cannot compete with paintings or sculptures. And yet it is precisely drawing which, of all the fine arts, achieves the greatest directness and intimacy. I do not know of any great engravers-etchers who, when drawing with the needle straight into the metal, and even when using the most instantaneous of techniques, the dry point—with the possibilities of reworking and retouching the plate— could approach the spontaneous sketch in all its mysterious freshness. Compare the studies for prints of any master, and in every case you will realize that the "aroma" of intercommunion between the hand of the artist and the paper, the drawing's musical tempo, key, pitch, and other elements (including the textural vibration or flowing of the line itself, the surface of the pencil or ink particles) have been lost. In truth, even the most vigorous etchings of Rembrandt and Goya added nothing to the expressivity of their preparatory drawings; on the contrary, when placed beside the original "scribbles and scratches," they may appear artificial and even lifeless. The same is true of many paintings, and I personally wish that Rubens and Raphael, for example, had almost never painted, but only drawn. It is hard to find a poor drawing of Rubens, the great draughtsman, yet there are many hundreds of bad paintings. And the paintings of Raphael's singing hand seldom found the intellectual grace and spirituality of his drawings. How happy were the old masters of the Orient whose paintings were also their brush sketches! Without using any other color than black, the Chinese, Korean, and Japanese artists carried to its acme a great colorist conception. I say all of this to excuse limiting my discussion of Hermann Talvik's work to his drawings: he is, among other things, a very skillful and productive painter, watercolorist, etcher, lithographer, linoleum-and-woodcut practitioner, book illustrator, and designer of stained glass.

2

In 1940, when he was thirty-four years old, Hermann Talvik saw the Soviets enter Estonia and lived through the period of horror and butchery that followed. Having received academic training in Estonia, Finland, and France, he was at the time of the Soviet invasion a successful art teacher. In his own work, of an introspective nature, Talvik was predominantly a formalist of the Nordic type, interested in still life and landscape, although already in his earliest productions concealing some unearthly forces. Also perceptible in the distant beginnings of his creativity was a cubist "decomposition," but the strong and varied gray colors, permeated with innate lyricism, prevailed over an intelligent commitment to the reality of shapes and space. The graphic artist Talvik began as a linearist and romantic realist, applying to his religious themes and motives a clean and gentle contour style without indication of space, light, or color. But the trauma of disaster and death under the Soviet occupation and the ensuing German-Soviet war shattered the rigid traditional *ordre et clarté* of Talvik's aesthetics, and after his escape in 1944 over the sea to Sweden he moved in his religious compositions and still lifes toward greater abstraction. The chaste melodic line of his early graphic works became nervous and fragmented, coupled with a dynamic reconstitution of the phenomenological aspects of nature through the sometimes ruthless light of the image and imagination. This is especially true of the compositions produced during the last two decades, which he has spent in isolation in the house built with his own hands in Swedish Lapland. There, among the storm-stunted, chimerical trees and the low-floating, beautiful, ghostly clouds (only to be seen in the far north), where open vistas extend to the horizon, delicately broken by barely elevated mountains, Talvik has given himself fully to the phantasmagoria of the Holy Scriptures (among them the Revelation of St. John the Divine), and even more to his own unworldly dreams and apparitions.

3

The eight unpublished and unexhibited charcoal drawings reproduced here are not directly connected with scriptural texts, but are testimonies of the artist's intense spiritual exercises, the fragments of a series of unique visions on which most of his late work is based. Some of these drawings, like "Death," "Binding Deeds," "The Grave of Joy," and "Prayer in Mourning," may be seen as preparatory studies for woodcuts or etchings. The others, especially "Outside of Time," demonstrate the artist's ability to seize a crucial moment in swift movement and render a tempestuous immediacy of creation. A definite design, or what the Italians call *modello,* in the first group is executed to give the artist an idea of his own intentions toward the final realization in another technique. In the second group, however, the drawing is an independent work of art. Yet the boundaries between the two groups are vague, since all of Talvik's drawings can be considered as ends in themselves. Built into the space of carefully planned geometrical figures, they display a dynamic rhythmical harmony of composition. The structure, the form as a whole, is premeditated, with an appearance of accidental "dislocation" of the axis created through subtle artifice.

Talvik is primarily a master of device. However impetuous his drawing may become, the form assumes substance through sustained contours of light and opaque relief as well as through accents of graphisms (line fragments or dark color patches) "scattered" across the paper. In "Zālam," for example, the surface is covered with a dense texture of feverish strokes—"writing in" the individual forms of ovals, spirals, circles, etc., organized in excited streams of vortexes. Everything is nonetheless held together by a strong rectangular frame, which restrains the play of both larger and smaller forms. Where others might leave a minute structural imperfection, Talvik persists to an ideal end. We observe an apparent stylistic conflict: movement is everything and movement is in everything, but in its finality it is an organic part of structure, of the time and space limitations themselves. The result is a kind of congenial exspressionistic classicism. The rapidly visualized sketch, with its loosely reined force of the unexpected, receives a clean, regular rhythm and becomes a highly wrought finished work. The open form is converted to a closed one, the *infinito* to *finito*.

There is another conflict, that of the chosen style and the content. While not lacking lightness and elegance in their refinement, Talvik's works bear the message of a heavily tormented soul. They convey at once the artistic assurance and the uncertainty of a pietist who is also an agitated original thinker. Unlike Rembrandt, whose religious work bears a perpetual mark of humility, or Blake, who in his happier simpler works exhibits a quality of angelic innocence, Talvik has eaten the fruit of the tree of knowledge and cannot return to the state of pure blessedness. For Rembrandt, who never makes allegorical or symbolic interpretations, the Bible is a profane, earthly book, the book of great images of simple man. For Talvik, however, as for Blake, the Scriptures and his own inspirations and inventions are raised to a superhuman solemnity; they are outgrowths of continual detachment from the things of this world.

4

In their mystic intensity, Talvik's manneristic and decorative drawings are often expressions of macabre genius. They reflect the sensuality, romanticism, and saturnine melancholy of his visions. Their enigmatic quality may give rise to singularly different judgments of him as a preacher and storyteller. Illumined by the fervor of faith necessary to the proper rendering of any spiritual subject, he abandons himself to his demonographic inspirations, creating his own apocrypha. The titles of the drawings dedicated to this apocrypha may have many meanings. "The Grave of Joy," of which Talvik made some forty variants, portrays man wrestling with the animal in himself, already wearing the evil feet of the beast. Or is this St. Peter transformed into the cock of Gethsemane? "Death," which depicts the destruction of the physical world, may also be the Fall of Lucifer, or it may echo the message of the Revelation of St. John: "And I saw another mighty angel come down from heaven." "Binding Deeds," representing the crucified Christ, may remind us of His binding sacrifice, or of the scene of Calvary in which Christ on the cross, His knees bent, cries: "My God, my God, why hast Thou forsaken me?" Or is it Christ triumphant, resurrected and praying for us and for our own resurrection? And what does the title "Eternal Fire" mean? Is it the story of Tobias, son of Tobiel, who was grievously tried by God and blinded—a story full of devils and demons and their oblique deeds? Or is it, as Talvik asserts, "simply" a union of two pairs of eyes, the eyes of God bursting in fire upon man, whose eyes are closed in worship? Sustained in slow movement, the most serene and the most poetically impressive of the eight drawings is that entitled "Prayer in Mourning." Viewing it for the first time, I was convinced of the presence of Martha and Mary.

Titles and explanations have no real importance, except for the iconographers. They may change with time and give currency to a number of new ideas. What is significant is the combination of philosophical and psychological qualities in Talvik's secret diary, in which religious emotions are brought to a level of aesthetic perfection. Although never so realistic as those of Goya, the dreams of Talvik are also *sueños*. The phantoms and deformed figures comprise the more striking features of these extraordinary productions. In this exploded world, Talvik often appears as a man bearing sin and penance, perhaps as a disobedient prophet or a disputing Jonah before the walls of Nineveh. He has embraced the center of the Gospel, but he may return home only as a prodigal son of the Dostoevskian sort, who must decide in free, fearful, and lonely anxiety where to place his belief. In the meantime he is still tried by temptations.

Talvik seems to be forever inwardly listening. Behind him, as behind Dostoevsky, we behold an angel (or a demon—a guardian demon?) who whispers the divine or satanic truth. Which one? Or perhaps I am mistaken. Talvik, as Thomas, may no longer need to touch the marks of Christ's wounds: having overcome his doubts, Thomas may soon fall to his knees, acknowledging, "My Lord and my God!"

Talvik's symbolism, personal and subjective and fraught with the emotions of terror and pity, may seem to some to be traditional, basically neo-Platonic, Biblical, and occult. But however strange and powerful, the content of Talvik's work is always subordinate to the form. What we see in it is the artistic singularity more than the message itself. We see the drawing as *drawing*: the coherence of proportions, the organic quality of line, the precise, daring design, the measured balance of the whole.—Is not content in art simply a part of form?

*Death*. Black-and-white charcoal drawing, 20″ x 15″. (Private collection) 1961

*Binding Deeds.* Black-and-white charcoal drawings, 17″ x 14″.
(Private collection) 1962

*The Grave of Joy.* Black-and-white charcoal drawing, 20" x 15". (Private collection) 1960

*Prayer in Mourning*. Black-and-white charcoal drawing, 20″ x 15″.
(Private collection) 1962

*Outside of Time*. Black-and-white charcoal drawing, 20″ x 15″.
(Private collection) 1961

*Zālam*. Black-and-white charcoal drawing, 20″ x 15″. (Private collection) 1961

*Eternal Fire*. Black-and-white charcoal drawing, 16½″ x 14″. (Private collection) 1963

*Lightning.* Black-and-white charcoal drawing, 20″ x 14″. (Private collection) 1961

# FOUR POEMS

ANNE WALDMAN

## SOME OF THE THINGS I SEE FOR YOU

1

Great & dramatic he is sprouting a truant
officer who's caught the kid (ram)
I watch Balzac light his candelabra
Or missed the kid she was gone so long
Ram against heart. That's funny
I am sometimes that child. Balzac
take your bath now
It's evening. Jupiter hangs in the north
east window
a western concert of cars below Jupiter
above the ground 5 floors now spend
the time shining dimes
or spend them quickly before they lose
value, car saddened by the bash.

I want you to walk in late like the German
director into his own movie
                              pierce my heart
lie down beside the insect & sleep
or stop the fuss of beautiful evaporated birds

2
This is the luxury of February
& the ease of language that grows
on the 6 window sills
green language or language of sun, cloud language
or language of bird
if seeing were the lighting I think it is.
Language, you are the glittering treasures locked in
the drawer he is pulling to get the whole
thing started
& we two live only to love that moment
they're found
    treasures of time
the wind sends you down the mountain to gather
remember? remember the way it smelled
your hand? & lift this one up to the light
to get a better look

I've mixed in the morning while you sleep
in the room like Paris the country
it's a capricious morning bath
not unlike the back of the mind
    perpetual & cloudy water

I wonder about the dolphin who danced
my part
when I dreamed that I slept & dreamed
that I dreamed
you are everywhere persuasive

    dazzling sun moaning in my past

PLUTONIUM POEM

Fuck Plutonium! Love it? Hate it?

We'll all be glowing for a quarter of a million years!

teeth glowing
underwear glowing
pages of words glowing
microfilm glowing
nails & knuckles glowing
sore kneecaps glowing
ankles in despair
antlers glowing
storm clouds glowing
hair follicles glowing
golden earlobes the better to hear you with
eyebrows glow
flaring nostrils glowing
wrinkles like streaks of lightning
clavicles glowing
dorsal angles of ribs glowing
thorax glowing
rolling pelvis glowing
hip joints glow
capillaries glow
ah the 3rd lumbar glowing in pain
eyeglass glowing poor sad monster eyeballs
REINCARNATED FOR A QUARTER OF A MILLION YEARS!


DEMON CHANT

demon in me, white woman demon in me
    moving moving see it moving through her

demon in me, black woman demon in me
    moving moving see it moving through her

demon of pride can't get my way today
    moving moving see it moving through her

demon of envy can't see my way today
    demon moving moving see it moving through her

there's traffic inside me
    traffic traffic see it moving through her

there's money in my brain
    money money see it moving through her

there's a monkey on my back
    monkey monkey see it jumping on her

I'm addicted to my appetite
    demon food demon demon

I'm addicted to my laziness
    lazy demon lazy sleeper

I'm in a hurry
    hurry demon make her hurry

I can't stop moving
    demon moving keep her moving

I can't sit still
    keep her hopping move her demon

my heart is hungry
    more more keep her hungry!

my bones are fearing
    death death demon

my face is fearing
    mirror death demon demon

let me hold onto you
    keep her hungry demon demon

let me see you
    give her the mirror demon demon

she's got breasts
   keep her guessing

she's got eyes like mine
   keep her musing

she's got teeth like mine
   keep her wild demon demon

I've got demons all around me
I've got demons coursing through me

fever demons
         hotter hotter!

icy demons
        freeze her freeze her!
my tongue is forked!   I'm split in 2!
        crazy crazy keep her crazy


## PREHENSILE

*After Chinese*


the light enfolds me
in its slants
you see I'm in my house
lying in a bed of aspen
studying being alone
miles from you, from anyone

icicles hang off the roof
the light crosses
my belly now
outside pine needles
bristle in the wind

actually shimmer
sometimes so metallic
and later on when
the light goes
over snow peaks
they're less distinct, flat

I'd like to say
it's not so terrible
when I start the fire
& see the light flicker
on my independence
but when my hands hold my head
bowed in resignation
I wonder

# ON THE EXTINCTION
# OF THE SPECIES

Regarding Six American Women in the 1960s

LINSEY ABRAMS

1

Everyone who met Isabel, from the meatcutter in the supermarket
to the maiden lady who lived next door, remarked at her astounding
beauty. "She's got real movie star looks," said the butcher. "Like a
miniature ballerina," the neighbor mused. For unlike other children,
who possessed a nascent loveliness, a preliminary outline for beauty,
Isabel had sprung from her mother full-blown. She was a Hedy
Lamarr in diapers. A Marilyn Monroe at twelve. Her father won-
dered if she'd looked like Cleopatra in the womb.

"I have amber eyes," said Isabel. "My waist is as narrow as a hat-
band. My lips are in the shape of a heart. My ears remind me of
sea shells I have picked up on the beach." In this way, Isabel came
to understand herself, the parts of her naked body like thoughts the
mirror gave voice to.

She read herself like a relief map. She was both the explorer and
the guide. She stuck out her tongue and measured it; she examined
the skin of her arm through a magnifying glass; using three hand
mirrors and a flashlight, she looked at the inside of her nostrils. She
touched herself everywhere; she wanted to know her own terrain;
she would be intimate with beauty.

These were the things Isabel didn't do: Skip down the sidewalk. Jump rope. Go to slumber parties. Instead: She learned to walk with her back arched and her shoulders thrown back. She taught herself not to blush, by first imagining herself in the most humiliating situations, by then regulating her short breaths and applying cool washcloths to her face. Looking into candle flames in her darkened bedroom, she practiced dilating and contracting her pupils at will. Further: Isabel never rode a bicycle. Isabel never ran as fast as she possibly could in gym class.

"How is my beautiful daughter today?" her father would ask at breakfast.

"————," Isabel might answer, for her words escaped him, he found he forgot to listen, watching the parting of her lips, the slow movement of her face.

Isabel the beautiful, he thinks. Isabel the daughter, and this confuses him, the idea of this recessive beauty, asleep for so long in his familial genes. Isabel the female, further. Isabel the expensive, he thinks . . . To her mother's mind, over toast, she is Isabel the beautiful. Likewise, Isabel the daughter. And, Isabel the young, Isabel the what-I-might-have-been.

Everywhere the two of them looked, they saw emanations of Isabel. Everything was either like Isabel or not like her at all, good for Isabel or potentially injurious. They saw Isabel's fate in the movies, her grown-up form in a bikini at the beach, her need for protein in the breakfast eggs. What they could not see clearly was Isabel herself, a Medusa of beauty, whose reflection they sought in the world around them. They knew their daughter by comparison, description: Isabel the . . .

Isabel Scotch-taped pictures of fashion models to her bedroom walls. She never wore her hair in a pony tail. If she'd wanted any friends, she would have had them. Ladies in flower-print dresses, who remembered the turn of the century, would stop her on the street to caress her cheek. Factory workers, traveling home on the evening bus, described to her their tasks on the assembly line. Boy Scouts followed her.

When her parents happened to look in the garage window one Saturday afternoon and found her sitting, shirtless, on the lap of the twenty-year-old assistant from the drugstore, they decided to send her to a boarding school.

"Boy crazy," said her mother, who in the flurry of the moment had not noticed that the two hands covering Isabel's breasts were her own.

It was possible to leave the boarding school on a week-end pass. Isabel made up the name of an aunt in a neighboring town, picked out an appropriate address from the telephone book, and went to a motel, where she used the two days to learn how to make love with a madras-jacketed boy she had met at a school dance.

"Hello?"

"I love you," he told her, long distance.

During the week, the boy had developed a fever. His eyes were yellowish; he felt a bit dry in the mouth. In class, when he picked up a book, he couldn't get the gist of even the most simple sentences. I've dallied with girls, he thought, in the long, over-the-wire pause. And now the tables are turned, the tables are turned. He saw round tables spinning, toplike, topsy-turvy, in the hands of poltergeists or Isabels. They made him dizzy. "Isabel?" he said, to rouse himself.

"Prove it," said Isabel, who'd been thinking about their love-making. In the mirror on the closet door, her body looked different to her. She saw it as having evolved, having taken on a new and special life of its own. Did her thighs have each a brain? Were her arms perceptive to the world around them? Were her nipples antennae? She was aroused watching herself as she talked to him, and she drew the telephone cord between her legs.

After she hung up, the boy sat in the phone booth wondering what he could send her to prove his love. He couldn't think of anything appropriate, grand enough, for Isabel. What can I send her? he asked into the mouthpiece of the telephone. A dozen roses, a mink coat (for the boy was wealthy), a gold bracelet all seemed paltry symbols of romance. He wanted to stun her, as she had stunned him. But it was hopeless. He thought of killing himself; he thought of withdrawing from school. Suddenly, being a man turned him weak. A single contestant, one warrior on the eve of battle, nevertheless he felt he represented a whole country of men. Like a David or a Goliath. Only he had to be both. In order to win Isabel, he thought, I must have cunning and I must have strength.

Later that month, Isabel received via parcel post her own portrait in oils, after a snapshot she had given the boy on their first meeting. Just as the floor was about to drop, he jerked his head from the noose, if temporarily. In time, the boy became a prototype, the first in a series who fell ill from the mysterious disease that was Isabel. The symptoms were always the same. The victims grew weakened, haphazard, crazy like syphilitics.

Isabel chewed men and spat them out. Anorexic, insatiable, she craved different tastes but could not swallow.

In college, Harry was the ninth person to ask her to marry him. His constitution was strong; he loved her perhaps a little less than the others; she took a chance. "Yes," she told him. And the disease lay within him, dormant. Isabel was allowed, at last, to dote on herself, like the larva which, when all nourishment is taken away, feeds greedily on its own posterior end.

"The market's up again," Harry told her at dinner, more than a year after their marriage.

"Do you like my blouse?" asked Isabel.

"Perhaps we can take a house on Long Island this summer," he said. "By the beach."

"I couldn't decide whether the peach was prettier . . . or the green. So I got both," she replied.

"You could move out for July and August," Harry said, "and I could join you on the week ends."

"Green for the bushes that line the edge of the beach," she said. "And peach for the color of the sand." So it was decided.

"A baby," he proposed one Sunday afternoon by the side of the pool. Isabel turned over onto her back.

"No," she said. She looked at her belly, transforming it like the earth, by mental effort, from flat to round. She tried to see the pool over the swollen bulge. Her body felt suddenly unwieldy, misshapen. She felt her waistline thicken. She thought of herself as two people. She was Siamese twins.

"Okay," he said. "We can wait a year or two. There's no rush."

Isabel imagined her body impregnated, stretched, and emptied. Was she just one beautiful link in a chain of descent? Was she to be sacrificed to generation? Harry stroked her shoulder and she pushed his hand away.

"Harry." She stared down at the concrete. "I don't want any children."

"We'd have the most beautiful babies in the world," he said. "Everyone has children. What do you mean, you don't want any kids?" He stood over her, blocking out the sun.

"I'll leave you," she said.

"Not ever?" he asked. For the first time, Harry, who'd instinctively known she'd never leave him for another man, was afraid of losing her. Inside, the sickness had started to spread.

"Never," said Isabel.

2

"Have you ever slept with a woman before?" Laurie asked her. Evelyn was pinned to the bed. For the long or the short count? Laurie wondered.

"No," said Evelyn. "Why, was I lousy?" Their bodies strained toward each other, like the two halves of a press, trying to push out all the air between them.

"I'm just the curious type," said Laurie. "Besides, I have a class in twenty minutes . . ."

"Life goes on."

". . . so I have to ask you about yourself in a straightforward manner."

"Shoot."

"How old are you?" Laurie asked.

"Twenty-two."

"Are your parents divorced?"

"No."

"Do you have a boyfriend?"

"Yes."

"Where did you get your good looks?"

"From my mother."

"Do you believe that the earth's atmosphere will be able to sustain life in forty years?"

"I don't know. I don't think so."

"Have you ever been to Europe?"

"Once."

"Are you as hungover as I am?"

"Yes."

"Do you want me to go to class?"

"No."

They stayed in bed all day. They made love. They took aspirin. They read each other passages from books. They had something to eat. They shared a beer. It was six o'clock:

"I have to go now," said Evelyn. "I really do."

"Life goes on."

"My roommate will think I'm dead," she said. They got dressed together. "And, since I'm not, George is going to kill me."

"I have a paper due tomorrow."

"If I don't practice the piano every day I have fantasies of my fingers falling off. Divine retribution, you know?"

"Well," said Laurie, pulling Evelyn to her, "you could practice twice as long tomorrow."

"And you could get an extension on your paper." So they took off each other's clothes and got back into bed. They made phone calls. They talked in long monologues—about their families, their ambitions, their past affairs. They made tea. They found a pair of scissors and trimmed each other's hair.

"Would you like bangs?" Laurie asked.

"Yes, please," said Evelyn.

They put on a record and danced. They lit up one cigarette at a time and chain-smoked. They drank brandy. They kissed.

"My life is full of surprises," said Evelyn, on the verge of sleep. "Here I am, happily, madly, in the arms of a woman."

"The woman, that's me," said Laurie. "Would you like to fly to Rio?"

"Would you like to hire a helicopter and tour Manhattan?" Evelyn asked.

"Would you like to walk across the Brooklyn Bridge?"

"Would you like to spend the week end at the Plaza?"

"Would you like to go to Jones Beach and bury each other in the sand?"

"Would you like me to move in with you?" Evelyn asked.

"Yes," said Laurie. "Only you're Jewish and the family wouldn't approve."

"Well at least we wouldn't have any children to worry about," said Evelyn. "That would start a religious war."

"Nope," said Laurie. "No children."


3

When Maureen's lover came over for the night, she would stop work early and cook him dinner. He visited infrequently enough that she didn't feel intruded upon, and in the first few months of their love-making, she even cooked his favorites: boiled live lobsters, veal Parmesan, crab soufflé.

"You're a terrific cook, Maureen," he'd tell her sincerely after finishing a meal, pushing his plate to the center of the table and reaching for a cigarette. "And a beautiful woman," he'd add.

"I'm fifty-two years old," she'd say. "And you're an ex-Green Beret who's looking for Mama. But you're a good lay, kiddo. And surely that's a good basis for any relationship between a man and a woman . . ."

"Maureen," he'd say to her. "You talk so tough. But there's a heart beating in there just the same. There's a heart . . ."

"Did they teach you to be tender in Nam?" she asked him. This was always her retort. "Listen, O'Reilly, I'm fifty-two years old," she'd tell him, "and I've had my combat training, too."

After dinner, she'd sketch him while he read the paper. Sometimes they drank too much, and then they'd just tumble into bed. Maureen could shout the house down when she was drunk.

"Don't be obscene," he said to her once.

"This is my house, O'Reilly," she told him, "and I'll do what I want in it. A woman's got to have a little space to breathe in, you know. So don't go practicing eminent domain around this establishment." Still, she hugged him as far as her arms would reach around his shoulders; she pushed her legs between his; she bit his chest. "You're just a kid," she said. "And you don't have a set of principles hanging around your neck yet. Be grateful."

Sometimes in the morning, he wondered if she hated him when they made love. Sometimes, when he'd gone off to work, she wondered if he knew how careful she was to keep him from falling in love with her.

During the day, Maureen painted seascapes and portraits of the fishermen who sailed out of the village.

"You make money off o' this?" one of them asked her, when she was a good deal younger.

"I do," she said.

"Are you famous?" he'd asked.

"No," said Maureen.

"I don't wonder," said her subject. "Your pickin' such pretty faces to paint . . . And it's no job for a lady hangin' around with the likes of us." But they got used to her.

"Hey Maureen. Maureen," they hailed her at the docks. "It's a nor'easter blowin' today." "The fish heard we were comin' yesterday and all swum to England." "Old Hazelton's down to the hospital." When he got out, Maureen drove him to the doctor's once a week for cancer treatment. "Have a drink, Maureen?" She'd sit with them at the end of the day, in their shacks, after the catch had been sold, drinking and sketching. Hermie was her favorite model.

"How's business, Hermie?" she'd ask. He had a hook in place of his left hand, severed in a car accident ("Bit off by a whale," he told her with a gleam in his eye).

"Not bad, today. Not bad." He wore green trousers and his teeth were tobacco-stained. "But it ain't like it used to be. The big trawlers are takin' over and it seems like we're using the fish up . . . Besides, they don't spawn like they used to." She liked best to draw his arms; each muscle was distinct under the skin. "So when's the weddin' day, Maureen?"

"Hermie, what a way to propose."

"Don't be kiddin' me like that . . ."

Sometimes they took her out beyond the breakwater at dawn. They usually saved a bit of the catch for her to take home. Once she wrote a seafood cookbook, sold it, and she threw a banquet at a local bar with the proceeds. They toasted her and sang "When Irish Eyes Are Smiling."

"Marry me," O'Reilly asked her one night. She perused the sketch in her lap, studying his features, his genitals.

"You caught me in a sentimental mood tonight," she told him, finally. "I almost said yes. But instead I'm going to do you a favor." She picked up his knit cap and put it on his head. "Go find yourself somebody who can meet you halfway," she said. She saw that he didn't understand. "Weigh anchor. The party's over, soldier," she said to make it easier.

"So you don't need me," he said. "Fucking all afternoon in those shacks with any fisherman who'll have you."

"That's right," she said. "Variety." He cuffed her out of the way and she let him go. She took out a bottle of Scotch and finished a seascape by morning. That afternoon she was tired and she took a nap, stretched out on the bed in blue jeans and an old workshirt, her hands variegated from the paints. The house was dark with the curtains drawn, colorless. Childless.

4

Unlike most of her women friends, Darlene wasn't adamant about a career. She threw pots sometimes and, when she did, sold them for a good price at a specialty store in San Francisco. This, she said it herself, was the extent of her ambition.

"I'm old-fashioned," she told her fiancé. "I want to have lots of children in a big old house, and I want to sit around and get fat and cook."

"The two often go hand in hand," he said. "I mean cooking and getting fat."

"You will have to make a lot of money," she told him. "I'll budget it carefully, but a large family takes capital."

"All right," he said. "But I'll only make a lot of money if you promise not to get fat."

"Strings attached. Already there's strings attached," she said. "It's true that a woman supported by her husband can't call her soul her own."

That night they watched the draft lottery on TV. The birthdays marched down the screen, in strict order, each one a batallion of innumerable young men to be called up or disbanded according to the number beside it. They watched: April 3—65

April 4—2

April 5—327 . . .

"Three twenty-seven!" they gasped. They threw themselves into each other's arms, they opened a bottle of wine, they smoked a joint, they set a date for the wedding, they forgot to look for Darlene's birthday. When Darlene's twin brother rang twenty minutes later, she and Eddie were arguing over what they would name their children.

"Richard? Is that you, Richard? Shit," said Darlene, remembering.

"Bad news," he said.

"We got a lousy number?"

"Thirty-four."

"Shit," she said, again.

"Well, I'm gonna go," he told her. She thought she might throw up. She leaned over the kitchen sink. After he hung up, she thought about being a woman. A woman didn't have to go to war. A woman didn't have to support herself. A woman didn't have to take responsibility for her own life. She didn't have to pull a grenade pin; she didn't have to figure out how to meet the mortgage payments; she didn't have to live beyond her reach. She thought of Richard napping in the jungle undergrowth; she went into the bedroom and looked at her own double bed. For a second she confused their genders. Which was which?

She called her mother up, but she was too stoned to say what she meant. They both started to cry.

"We could move to Canada," her mother said.

"Richard would never go, though."

"The men in this family are so stubborn," her mother said. "And unlucky, too. Every generation coming of age to go to war. World War I, your grandfather. Then your father in World War II. Uncle Milt in Korea, and now Richard. I just don't know . . ."

"Would you fight?" Darlene asked.

"I don't know," said her mother. "I never thought about it."

"And to think it's all in a number," said Darlene.

Darlene had jungle dreams. Her mother had jungle dreams. Tiny men with machetes entered their sleep, hacking at limblike foliage. Large birds turned into low-flying airplanes, dropping napalm eggs from above. Darlene dreamed she was barren. She dreamed she was her brother. She dreamed she had thirty-four children. She thought she was still dreaming when five months later the telegram arrived, saying that Richard's legs had been blown off. She watched the Western Union man walk down the front steps and into the street. By a land mine. He was recuperating in an army hospital.

When he was wheeled down the ramp from the airplane, Darlene made herself look at the place where his legs should have been. She would look at the little stumps when the empty trouser legs were pulled off, too. She wouldn't be a "woman" any more, because a "woman" didn't have to look.

"We'll see the best specialists there are," her mother said that night.

"They can't grow your legs back," said Richard.

"You can have something fitted," said Eddie.

At the wedding, because their father was dead, Richard escorted Darlene down the aisle in his wheelchair. It was awkward; there was hardly enough room for the two of them, but Darlene insisted.

The next day, on the airplane on the way to Mexico, she told Eddie that she wasn't sure she wanted any kids.

"Do we procreate to give our sons to armies?" she asked. "To give our daughters to the survivors just to make more babies?"

"At first it seemed to be all in a number," she said. "But it's not in the number, in the chance. It's in the world. And that means it's in us too . . . Parents? What kind of parents are content to leave a legacy of plastic limbs and wheelchairs and hopelessness?"

5

"We could get married," said her lover of five years.

"What good would getting married do?" she asked. She sat down on the couch with her head in her hands, her legs spread wide apart, as if she might try to suck the fetus out with her own breath.

"Then you could have it," he said.

"No I could not." She looked at him. "I absolutely could not. It has nothing to do with being married or not, you know that. Would you have it?" she asked him.

"That's an absurd question," he said.

"You think it's absurd because it applies to you, and you're a man so you don't know anything about these things. Well I'm a woman and I don't know anything about these things, either. Now do you see what the problem is?"

"Yes."

They had a couple of drinks at the bar around the corner. The semidark exaggerated sounds: the reedy melodies of the juke box, glasses touching, human voices. Normally she liked the atmosphere, but tonight she found it oppressive, opiated. The best way, she knew, to think things through was to project all potentialities into daylight. (Making it with a stranger in the daylight. Confronting her mother with a lie in the daylight. Leaving him in the daylight.) She saw herself in the sunshine, giantlike, towering over a small child. They rode a bus together; she held its hand; they went walking through Central Park Zoo. The child had a bright red snowsuit, but it had no face. Even so, everything in the fantasy was the child. The child made her crazy.

"I'm going to have an abortion," she said.

"It seems like the smartest thing to do," he said.

"It is the smartest thing. Of course it is. But you can't do it on account of that," she said. She felt better having said this, having thought it. "I'm going to sit here for five minutes and try to imagine who that kid might be," she told him. "If I can still abort it after that, I will." Conscientiously, she looked at the people in the bar: people who drank too much, people who were good dancers, people who spoke to one another with sincere faces. Someone who sat, in a coat, on the corner stool at the bar; someone whose eyes were wild with being in love with the person whose back was to her; two people who kept clinking glasses, toasting each other with their hands, in the language of the deaf. These lives, good and bad, as she imagined them, made her feel ashamed. She found the child in all of them.

Tears diluted her drink. The people became indistinct.

"The problem is," she said to him, "sometimes I can't even drag myself out of bed in the morning because the day's already there ahead of me, waiting. Sometimes I can't even look at you. Sometimes I can't bear to be in the same skin with myself. Me . . . A mother?"

"Jesus," he said. He watched her put the drink to her lips. "And it might be dangerous, too."

"No, no," she said. "A lot of good doctors are doing them now because everybody knows it will be legal in a year or two." She lit one of his cigarettes and blew tiny smoke rings. "I think Fran can find me somebody. But they're expensive."

"Forget about that."

She went to one doctor who referred her to another who would do it. He felt for the fetus inside her and found it. She payed him the four hundred dollars gladly, wanting to think about it as some business deal.

In his office one evening, after hours, the doctor inserted a plastic tube filled with chemical into her uterus, and thirty-six hours later, the bleeding started. She called into work, sick; she lay down on the bed; and when he came home unexpectedly that afternoon, she sent him into the other room. She thought of primitive women who insisted on being by themselves during labor. Was this pain she felt the same as that of women giving birth? The pain was like a helix that encapsulated her, like a cocoon that hatched blood.

"I'm going to call the doctor," said her lover from a great distance.

"I'm all right. This is what's supposed to happen," she told him. She felt a wet cloth on her forehead. The pain was like being drunk. She vomited. The room spun like a centrifuge, trying to separate her from the baby.

When she awoke, she looked down between her legs at the red sheet and the tiny, flesh-colored fetus, two months old and dead. Nine hours had passed.

The bleeding continued for four weeks, and after that she tried to forget it, to flow away from herself as the blood had. On the week ends she went to afternoon movies, she often worked overtime, she called friends she'd been meaning to get in touch with for months.

# INTERVIEW

GÁBOR GÖRGEY

*Translated from the Hungarian by Jascha Kessler*

1
I'm fine, thanks.
Teeth
in good shape.
Some hair, yes. I hope
it stays on, who knows.
Yes, family.
Naturally—why, don't I look
like a man who loves life?
It's brushed me, twice.
Vitality, and style.
Size 12. Yes, a little large.
I've quit, finally.
I wouldn't know.
This and that.
Here and there.
Lots.
Have a smoke? Coffee?
Any other questions, Miss?

2
Visions? Havent any.
Shoving on step by
step through some
inimical stubborn
jungly stuff as sly
and tricky as a rogue beast,
clawing it out of the ground
down to the bone
I make what I can of it.
In childhood, once upon a time,
I had visions, lots of them,
poetic, the real thing.
But it stopped, just like that,
when I started writing poems.
Visions. What I get's the old shaft.


3
Favorite dish?
If you could pour
some of that brisk-smelling
mushroom sauce over
the High Tatra and garnish it
with a crisp salad of Maytime
pastures awash in a dressing
of fat dew—I'd gladly dine on that.


4
Well now when the rooftree
caved in on me,
we thought at first
it had to be woodworms,
then some unclassified
European species of termite—but
the fault was simple,
natural decay.
My headwound's healed,
finally.
More or less.

5
Our forefathers?
When they were building
Sumatra City
these tigers and antelopes
hopped into their heads.
There's supposed to be a Mongolian still alive,
a wonderworking shaman somewhere
who could purge them,
but they've never had time
to go for the cure
because of all their congresses
and official parades.
So the tigers have come down to us,
and the antelopes, their feed.
Still and all, that grand Sumatran
housing project was neat;
it's a pity they couldnt get it finished
and the city of the future
was swallowed by the jungle's
green fire.
O good old days.
O heroes of yore.


6
Maybe those monstrous
yoni-forms can never
be forgotten.
The herd clatters over
the feet of the tit-towers.
Worships milling
in the acorn groves.
Thighs in the iron grip
of ecstasy.
Tranced continuum.
But on the other isle
those who saw with refined fear
what was happening to love here
felt their manhood
shriveling,

so scared not even Circe
could have stroked their fountain up.
That's it. We can choose between
boys grunting in rapture
or those with the withered balls.
Because it's hard, oh hard, hard
to be Odysseus clearing out
in his black ship, Miss.

7
Snow? I like it, yes.
Sometimes though it seems
to sort of blend in
with the Sahara.
Discrimination's so difficult
these days, dont you think?

8
What I think of sleighs—
since you've asked me, Miss—
the sleigh's a useful vehicle
in winter.
And the bell
on the horse's neck is
perfectly ravishing.
But watch it there: when you coast down
from the shepherd's lofty, cheesy hut
to the café,
keep a fur hat and good sheepskin handy.
Because up there the frost's
tolling.

9
That rock-artist howler?
Sure I know him! We chatted
for hours the other day.
He told me extraordinary
things about Early Medieval Russian
icon-painting.

10

I'll tell you about that too.
I was led
to a girl's boudoir
packed with masked bandits.
I had to rescue the virgin
who gratefully gave herself to me
in that pink and white decor.
when it was over we went
for a ride, a cloud of lace floating
fragrant on the horse's rump.
Finally we rowed, I think,
on a pointillist pond.
So that's what happened
to me in the Jeu de Paume.


11

They sawed some
left-over gaslights
in half.
The iron torsos
line the embankment
where lovers stroll.
They are kissing, and
from the black, cavernous stumps
the hovering, sweet, insidious stench
of gas surrounds them.


12

The racket of that locust-colored
Diesel train running along
the other shore of the lake
can be heard even from here.
It's coming round the bay
one fine day
right to our house. O, Miss,
why wont you take it from me:
a man cant see those tracks coming
till they run through his room
right over my bed?

13
Like linens stacked
with love's fragrant lavender
in grandmother's cupboard—
in the terminal wards
old age homes
despair, loneliness
catarrhal laughter
vitamin deficiency, bedwettings,
fiftyseven varieties of cancer
lined up, neatly catalogued.
Isnt it adventurous of us
to lay our doddering folks
away so scrupulously in lavender?

14
These bugs live
only a couple of hours.
They've got it made, though.
Excavator-legs, prismatic lenses,
radar-sensors and a perpetual motion
sexual subsystem.
With supersonic wings extolling
nature's sophisticated engineering.
Naturally, because millions of years
of labor have been invested
in each
bug,
born in glory
just to drop dead in an hour or so.

15
You see this little saw:
my tamed beastie.
When we go hunting
it perches on my fist,
and when I release it
prey falls from its path.
When we're tired out
we dont bother counting
the dry branches and twigs strewn about:
it goes to sleep on its nail,
my steel-taloned bird.

16
What I admire?
Concentration of soul
giving you the strength,
for example, to burn yourself alive.
And the iron calm
of the citizen in me
listening to the 8 a.m. news
and cracking the second
soft-boiled egg
so essential for his existence.

17
It's a big fat hypothesis, of course.
But well constructed, even
a Martian could see that.
I admit there are other
palatable hypotheses, but
I'm not about to kowtow
groveling in the dust
with the rest of them
every time the tribe's adored totem-face
stares at me.
My backbone's no thrilling conductor
of cultural currents—
in fact I'm turned off:
because these days it's not just
connoisseurs of the primitive
but conquerors too who
ooze goodwill.

18
You cant mean that.
Absolutely ridiculous.
I dont believe my ears.
Maybe I got it wrong.
You wouldnt mind repeating what you said?
So I hear you right! I'm
just appalled, Miss.

19

Were you there, too? You got to see
that fabulous well, didn't you,
where tourists take the plunge
from the edge, immersing themselves,
doing the antique abyss?
A marble phallus
broke off under me and I lost
interest in the whole trip,
but take my word for it
I was the only tourist
with that kind of luck,
and I brought home an empty soul.
That indefatigable American woman though,
what a thirst for culture she had, and
what a splash she made, ye gods!

20

Those pencils you're taking notes with
are the best there are.
Carried only by that hole-in-the-wall place
between Scylla and Charybdis.
You reach the overhanging cliff
by water, in a skiff,
and the sea's monster fins thrash
so madly here
even the saltiest pirates
wont go out unless
you come up with a
really heavy tip.
But if you do make it
in a weathered skiff
and get out alive—
you'll find the best pencils
on earth
there.

21

All this, to go it alone,
for its own sake, and mine?
For what,
to perfect myself?
Polish it off
like an honor student
with a 4-point average?
Show
what great time I ran,
the champ, me?
To pick up a cum laude metaphysical
degree later on?
So as to jeer triumphant
at the rest
who couldnt swing it?
Even though the job
demands
personal dedication
you cant get your kicks out of it
unless we're in it together.
Only a stone lives alone.


22

Nice to hear that, Miss.
I do make a point
of shaving close, yes.
It brings in this sort
of mini-success, among others.
But after razoring it clean,
deep-rubbing my wincing face—
how the lotion bites—
behind its contented grin
a bit of that endless rope of pearls
stringing out through the earth
exposes itself:
the Homo Sapiens mandible.

23
Yes, memory's the problem.
What I dont recall, just
isnt. Life after death
will only be perfect
(I mean, refined from earthly dross)
if they can sublimate my
dematerialized matter
out of all recollection.
If, however, from the ranks of tremulant souls
I cant pick my mother out—
because memory's gone—
let me ask you, Miss, where's the point in it?
Happiness?
Listen, all it takes
with this grace-contraption
is losing that one single
screw
and my ramshackle residence
of lights and shadows
tumbles down.
Happiness, it seems, is merely
a malfunction in the rhythm
of horror.

25
There it is.
Of course it is.
If it werent, it couldnt be.
But since it is,
it must be,
and if it must
it certainly
is.

# HOW I BECAME A SHADOW

*An excerpt from the novel-in-progress Narrow Rooms*

JAMES PURDY

How I Became a Shadow, how I live in the defile of mountains, and how I lost my Cock.
 By Pablo Rangel.
 Gonzago is to blame. He said, "That rooster is too good for a pet. He belongs in the cockfight. You give him to me, you owe me favors. I am your cousin. Give him up."
 "Never, Gonzago." I replied. "*Nunca.* I raised the little fellow from almost an egg. I never render him to you, *primo.*"
 "Shut your mouth that flies are always crawling in. Shut up, you whelp, when I command. That cock is too good for a pet. Hear me. You will give him up, and we will both make money. You bellyache, you say you are always broke, and then when the chance comes to make something you tell your cousin to go hang his ass up to dry. No, Pablo, listen good. The cock is as good as mine because of all the favors I done you, remember. Hear me. I am going to come take him and will fetch you another cock to take his place. Then I will enter your cock at the fight and we will get rich."
 "I will not render him," I told Gonzago. "I will keep my pet by me forever. You are not man enough anyhow to take him from me. If Jesus Himself come down from the clouds and said, 'Pablo, I re-

quire you to render me your cock as an offering,' I would reply, 'Jesus, go back and hang again on the cross, I will not render my pet, die, Jesus, this time forever.' "

"Ha, Jesus, always Him," Gonzago snorted. "As if He cared about your cock or whether he fights or don't fight. You fool, even your shit isn't brown. You were born to lose. But I will teach you yet. You will not order your cousin about just because you have no wits and need others to watch out for you . . . Hear me . . . Tonight I will come for the cock. Hear? Tonight, for tomorrow is the cock fight, and we will win, Pablo. I have been teaching your Placido to fight while you were waiting table at the big American hotel. Ha, you did not even notice? See, Placido is ready."

"Ah, so that is why he is so thin and don't eat, evil Gonzago . . . Never, never say you will take him though . . . Look into my eyes, cousin, what do you see there, look good."

"I see nothing in your eyes but stubborn pigheaded pride. Starve to death, why don't you, see if I care. Go with your ass to the wind forever, or die and be dead forever like Jesus . . . But I will take your cock when I want to on account of you owe me your life, you owe me money for your keep since a boy, you *owe owe owe!*"

"Nothing, Gonzago. I owe you nothing, and won't never give up what I don't owe for. Kill me if you want to . . . Here is my machete my grandfather passed on to me. Take it and cut me in two, see if I care!"

That night, Gonzago returned with a big burlap sack with an iron piece that shut over the mouth. He took Placido from his little warm box. My pet gave out piteous little cries as he was grasped, I rushed over to him, but Gonzago had put him already in the sack, and run like the wind and got in his truck and drove off to the cock ring.

I followed on foot. I did not know what I did. I smoked something, smoked it many times. I lost track of time smoking it. Then there I was at the fight sitting in the front row of seats, watching through blue clouds of smoke, not knowing yet one rooster from another.

Then I saw the light of my life come forward, the pet I all alone had raised and whose name I called: "Placido! Placido! *Amor mío!*" I yelled and shouted until the police came and took me outside and clubbed me for kicking them. I fell down on the curb and talked to its cold stones.

After the air revived me, I stole back into the arena. Gonzago stood in the center of a knot of men. "You can have your pet back now," he spoke to me inhaling on a cigar with an end like a volcano. "Over there, *primo*," he pointed, "behind the piled-up folding chairs and the flag."

I went there and looked down on the ground where he had pointed.

At first I see nothing, just earth and a few cigar wrappers. Then I made out his form at last. He was all wings spread on the black soil, but with no eyes. Placido had no eyes! But I knew him still by his gold and red feathers, and his pretty head. But no eyes!

I waited until I got possession of myself, and my heart had quit thundering in my ears. Then I came back to Gonzago. I smiled. Gonzago relaxed. "I invite you to a drink, Pablo." "Fine," I agreed.

We went to the saloon. Gonzago ordered the best tequila, he paid, he ordered again, the money showered from his hands covered with rings.

When he was feeling his liquor, I pretended friendship and patted him. "Gonzago," I said, "you are a very clever man, and have my good at heart."

"*Gracias, primo*," he said, and he relaxed some more.

"Because of that," I went on, "I want to share again with you. I have another cock you do not know about. A great scrapper and bigger than Placido."

"Is that so?" Gonzago wondered.

"Yes, *primo*, come closer, please, and I will show him to you. This one is a winner. Here, here, look, Gonzago," and I uncovered the little machete I had hidden under my coat.

I cut swiftly like a parcel of winds across Gonzago's unprotected brow. I reddened his eyes with one blow of my machete after another, I cut his eyes to holes like those that were left in Placido's head.

"Placido, *amor*, rest happy, Placido, be avenged. Die, Gonzago, with blind *ojos*, die, blind eyes!"

Then I ran to the mountains where I move like hawks or a mountain cat, or vesper winds. But I keep Placido's feathers against my heart. I live in the defile of mountains. I am called Shadow.

# FIVE POEMS

BOBBIE LOUISE HAWKINS

## DEPTHS AND HEIGHTS AND SWEET RED MELONS

in summertime
The bottom fell out of the market
over all the plains where melons
weren't worth the picking

Me and Donald-Gene walked the rows
lost in that field of bypassed crops

Kid's eye level on a clear day
in hot sun
Far as the eye can see melons
baking ripe

Biggest watermelon patch
in all the wide world

Donald-Gene and me in overalls
got sick day after day walking
the rows eating watermelon hearts

Exacting and perfectionist
we did it this way:

> Pick a watermelon up
> to waist high and drop it
> when it's ripe it breaks
> right open so the heart
> sits high
> on the seedy mess of the rest

One for him
One for me

I swear nobody ever
had it better


## WHAT IS THAT GESTURE . . .

What is that gesture quiet women make

in late afternoon
as the sun shifts to its loveliest
length of light

It is a way the fingers and the mouth
go together

They lift their hand and
put one or two fingers over their lips
as if to feel that silence they keep
in place

or as consolation
mouth lonesome
fingers lonesome
touch for consolation

A long slant of sunlight falls
athwart thought

and those women make that gesture


## IT'S LIKE . . .

It's like a Restoration novel
where
    So-and-So learns

that
    Miss So-and-So has
    *legs*

and will
use them

    on occasion


## ENDLESSLY . . .

endlessly endlessly coming out
through green leaves

all the bushes all the trees
at all the levels

the leaves are green
above and over

face shoulders knees
my feet step on them

all the leaves are green
endlessly coming out of that green wood

leaves clinging to their branches
fill the air I'm going past

that thickest forest
sweet leaves float green

I push through endlessly
coming out


A WESTERN . . .

A western desert town

Dust-devils whirl over there
    beyond the livery stable's corral

Two heros hit the street
    wearing black and blue
    walking slow and wary

    hands hover like birds

Every night there's
    a full and orange moon
    for the hero who came through

# THE SAXIFRAGE FLOWER
# (THE ROCKBREAKER)

OCTAVIO PAZ

*Translated from the Spanish by Donald D. Walsh*

*For James Laughlin*

In the first third of our century a change took place in the literatures of the English-speaking world that equally affected verse and prose, sensitivity and syntax, imagination and prosody. The change— similar to those that occurred in about the same period elsewhere in Europe and Latin America—was essentially the work of a handful of poets, almost all Americans. In this group of forerunners William Carlos Williams has a place that is both central and singular: unlike Pound and Eliot, he preferred to bury himself in a small city on the outskirts of New York rather than exile himself, as they did, in London and Paris; unlike Wallace Stevens and E. E. Cummings, who also decided to stay in the United States but who were cosmopolitan spirits, Williams sought from the beginning a poetic Americanism. Indeed, as he explains in a fine book of essays, *In the American Grain*, America is not a reality given to us but something that among us all we make with our hands, our eyes, our minds, and our lips. The reality of America is material, mental, visual, and above all, verbal: whether he speak Spanish, English, Portuguese, or French, the American man speaks a language distinct from the original European. More than a reality that we discover or create, America is a reality that we speak.

William Carlos Williams was born in Rutherford, New Jersey, in 1885. His father was English and his mother Puerto Rican. He studied medicine at the University of Pennsylvania. There he met Pound—a friendship that would last his whole lifetime—and the poet H. D. (Hilda Doolittle), who fascinated the two young poets. After obtaining his medical degree and after a short period of pediatric studies in Leipzig, he settled down for good in Rutherford in 1910. Two years later he married Florence Herman. A lifetime marriage. Also for life was his double devotion to medicine and poetry. Although he lived in the provinces, Williams was not a provincial: he was immersed in the artistic and intellectual currents of our century, he traveled to Europe several times and was a friend of English, French, and Spanish-American poets. His literary friendships and enmities were varied and intense: Pound, Marianne Moore, Wallace Stevens, Eliot (whom he admired and disapproved of), E. E. Cummings, and other younger figures like James Laughlin and Louis Zukofsky. His influence and friendship were decisive on Allen Ginsberg and also on the poetry of Creeley, Duncan, and the Englishman Tomlinson. (Poetic justice: a young English poet and very English—praised precisely by one who practiced all his life a kind of poetic anti-Anglicism and never tired of saying that the American language was not really English.) In 1951 he suffered his first paralytic attack, but he lived for another twelve years, fully devoted to a literary activity of unusual fecundity: books of poetry, a translation of Quevedo, memoirs, lectures, and readings of his poems all over the country. He died on the fourth of March, 1963, in Rutherford, the place where he had been born and spent his whole life.

Williams's work is vast and varied: poetry, novel, essay, theatre, autobiography. The poetry has been collected in four volumes: *Collected Earlier Poems* (1906–39), *Collected Later Poems* (1940–50), *Pictures from Breughel* (1950–62), and *Paterson* (1946–58), a long poem in five books. In addition, a slender volume of prose poems that at times makes one think of the automatic texts that Breton and Soupault were writing at about the same time: *Kora in Hell: Improvisations* (1920). But when he appropriated a poetic form invented by French poetry, Williams changed it and transformed it into a method of exploration of language and of the subterranean strata of the collective soul. *Kora in Hell* is a book that could have been written only by an American poet, and it should be read in the perspective of a later book which is the center of Williams's Americanism, his *ars poetica: In the American Grain* (1925). I shall not concern myself here with his novels, short stories, and theatrical works. It will suffice to say that they are extensions, irradiations of his poetry. The frontier between prose and verse, always hard to trace, becomes very tenuous in this poet: his free verse borders on prose, not written prose but spoken prose, with everyday language; and his prose is always rhythmic, like a coast bathed in poetic waves—not verse but the verbal surge and resurge that is the creator of verse.

Ever since his first writings, Williams revealed his distrust of ideas. It was a reaction against the symbolist aesthetic shared by most poets of that time (let us recall López Velarde) and in which, in his case, were combined American pragmatism and his profession as a doctor. In a famous poem he defined his search: "To compose: not ideas but in things." Except that the things are always beyond, on the other side: the "thing itself" is intangible. Thus Williams does not depart from things but from sensation. But in turn, sensation is shapeless and instantaneous; one can not construct or create anything with pure sensation; the result would be chaos. Sensation is amphibious; it unites us to and simultaneously separates us from things. It is the door through which we enter into things but also through which we emerge from them to realize that we are not things. In order that sensation yield to the objectivity of things sensation itself must be transformed into things. Language is the agent of change: sensations become verbal objects. A poem is a verbal object, a fusion of two contradictory properties: the liveliness of the sensation and the objectivity of the things.

Sensations become verbal things through the operation of a force that to Williams is not essentially different from electricity, steam, or gas: the imagination. In some reflections of 1923 (included among the poems of the first edition of *Spring and All* as "displaced prose"), Williams says that imagination is "a creative force that makes objects." The poem is not a reflection of the sensation or of the thing. The imagination does not represent, it produces. Its products are poems, objects that did not previously exist in reality. The poetic imagination produces poems, pictures, and cathedrals as nature produces pine trees, clouds, and crocodiles. Williams twists the neck of traditional aesthetics: art does not imitate nature, it imitates its creative procedures. It does not copy its products but its mode of production. "Art is not a mirror reflecting nature, rather, the imagination rivals the compositions of nature. The poet becomes nature and works like nature." It is incredible that our critics have not noticed the extraordinary similarity of these ideas with those which, during the same years (or strictly speaking a little before) Vicente Huidobro proclaimed in declarations and manifestos. Of course, we are dealing with ideas that appear in many poets and artists of the period (for example, in Reverdy, who introduced Huidobro to modern poetry), but the resemblance between the North American and the Latin American is impressive. Both *invert*, almost in the same terms, Aristotelian aesthetics and *convert* it into the modern era: the imagination, like electricity, is an agent, and the poet is the agent of transmission.

The poetic theories of Williams and Huidobro's "creationism" are twins, but enemy twins. Huidobro sees in poetry a hemologue of magic and he wants, like the primitive shaman who *makes* rain, to make poetry; Williams conceives the poetic imagination as an activity that complements science and rivals it. Nothing is farther from magic than Williams. In a moment of childish egotism, Huidobro said: "the poet is a little God," a phrase that the North American poet would not have approved. Another difference: Huidobro tried to produce verbal objects that would not be imitations of real objects and that would even deny them. Art as a means of escaping from reality. The title of one of his books is likewise a definition of his proposal: *Squared Horizon*. An impossible attempt: it is enough to compare the pictures of the abstract painters with the images that we get from microscopes and telescopes to realize that we cannot get outside of nature. To Williams artists—it is significant that he depends upon and draws inspiration from the example of Juan Gris—*separate* the things of the imagination from the things of reality: cubist reality is not the table, the cup, the pipe, and the newspaper of reality; it is *another* reality, no less real. This *other* reality does not deny the reality of real things: it is *another* thing which is simultaneously the *same* thing. "The mountain and the sea of a picture of Juan Gris," says Williams, "are not mountain and sea but a picture of mountain and sea." The poem-thing is not the thing: it is another thing that exchanges signs of intelligence with the thing.

The nonimitative realism of Williams brings him close to two other poets: Jorge Guillén and Francis Ponge. (Again, I am pointing to coincidences, not influences.) A line of Guillén defines his common repugnance for symbols: "the little birds chirp with no design of grace." Do the grace and the design disappear? No: they enter surreptitiously into the poem, without the poet's noticing it; the "design of grace" is not now in the real birds but in the text. The poem-thing is as unattainable as the poem-idea of symbolist poetry. Words are things, but things with meaning. We cannot put an end to the sense without putting an end to the signs, which is to say, to the language itself. And more than that: we should have to put an end to the universe. All the things that man touches become impregnated with sense. In the view of man, things exchange being for sense: they do not exist, they signify. Even "not having any sense" is a way of emitting sense. The absurd is one of the extremes to which sense comes when it examines its conscience and asks itself: what sense does sense make? The ambivalence of sense: it is the crack through which we enter into things and through which the being escapes from them.

Sense undermines the poem ceaselessly; it wants to reduce its reality as a sensitive object and a unique thing to an idea, a definition, or a "message." In order to defend the poem from the ravages of sense, poets accentuate the material side of language. In poetry, the physical properties of the sign, sonorous or visual, are not less important but more important than the semantic properties. Or rather: sense goes back to sound and becomes its servant. The poet works on the nostalgia that the significance has for the signifier. In Ponge this operation comes about through the constant play between prose and poetry, fantastic humor and common sense. The result is a new being: the *objeu*. Nevertheless, we can make fun of the sense, scatter it and pulverize it, not destroy it: integral or in lively and waggy fragments, like sections of a serpent, sense reappears. The creative description of the world is transformed, on one hand, into the criticism of the world (the moralist Ponge)—and on the other hand, into *proème* (the *précieux* Ponge, a kind of Baltasar Gracián of objects). In Guillén the celebration of the world and of things flows into history, satire, elegy: again, sense. Williams's solution to the amphibious nature of language—words are things and they are sense—is different. He is not a European with a history behind him and already established but ahead of him and still to establish. He does not correct poetry with the morality of prose nor does he convert humor into a master teaching resignation to song.

On the contrary: prose is the soil where poetry grows, and humor is the spur of the imagination. Williams is a sower of poetic seeds. The American language is a buried grain that will bear fruit only if it is given water and sun by the poetic imagination.

A partial reconciliation, always partial and provisional, between the sense and the thing. The sense—criticism of the world in Guillén and criticism of the language in Ponge—becomes in Williams an active power at the service of things. Sense *makes* sense, is the midwife of objects. Williams's art seeks "through metaphor to reconcile the people and the stones," American man and his landscape, the talking human and the mute object. The poem is a metaphor in which objects talk and words cease to be ideas in order to become sensitive objects. The eye and the ear: the heard object and the sketched word. As to the first, Williams was the teacher and friend of the so-called "objectivists," Zukofsky, Oppen; as to the second, of the Black Mountain group, Olson, Duncan, Greeley. The imagination not only sees: it hears; it not only hears: it speaks. In his search for the American language, Williams finds (hears) the basic measure, a meter of variable foot but with a triadic accentual base. "We know nothing," he says, "save the dance: the measure is all we know." The poem-thing is a verbal, rhythmic object. Its rhythm is the transmutation of the language of a people. Through language Williams leaps from things and sensations into the world of history.

*Paterson* is the result of these preoccupations. Williams passes from the poem-thing to the poem-system-of-things. A system single and multiple: single like a city that would be a single man, multiple like a woman that would be many flowers. *Paterson* is the biography of a city in the industrial area of eastern United States and the story of a man. City and man merge in the image of a waterfall that plunges, with a deafening sound, from the stone mouth of the mountain. Paterson was founded at the foot of that mountain. The falls and the language itself, the men who never know what they say and who always go in search of the sense of what they say. The falls and the mountain, the man and the woman, the poet and the man, the pre-industrial and the industrial age, the incoherent noise of the falls and the search for a measure and a sense.

*Paterson* belongs to that poetic genre invented by modern North American poetry and which oscillates between the *Aeneid* and the *Treatise of Political Economy,* the *Divine Comedy* and journalism. Vast collections of fragments, the most imposing example of which are the *Cantos* of Pound. All these poems, possessed as much by desire to speak the American reality as by the desire to create it, are the contemporary inheritance of Whitman, and all of them, in one way or another, tend to fulfill the prophecy of *Leaves of Grass*. And in a certain way they do fulfill it, but they fulfill it negatively. Whitman's theme is the incarnation of the future in America. A marriage of the concrete and the universal, of the present and the future: American democracy is the universalization of European national man and his taking root in a particular land and society. The particularity lies in the fact that that society and that land are not a tradition but a present exploded toward the future. Pound, Williams, and even Crane are the reverse of that promise; what their poems show us are the ruins of that project. Ruins no less grandiose and impressive than the others. The cathedrals are the ruins of Christian eternity, the stupas are the ruins of Buddhist vacuity, the Greek temples, those of the *polis* and geometry, but the great American cities and their suburbs are the living ruins of the future. It is in those immense industrial scrap heaps that the philosophy and morality of progress have ended. With the modern world comes to an end the titanism of the future, in the fact of which the titanisms of the past—Incas, Romans, Chinese, Egyptians—seem childish castles of sand.

The poem of Williams is complex and uneven. Beside magic or realistic fragments of great intensity there are long disconnected selections. Written in the face of and at times in opposition to *The Waste Land* and the *Cantos,* he reveals the effect of his polemic with these two works. In this lies his principal limitation; a reading of him depends on other readings, so that the judgment of the reader unavoidably becomes a comparison. The vision that Pound and Eliot had of the modern world was rather somber. Their pessimism was steeped in feudal nostalgia and in precapitalist concepts; therefore their just condemnation of money and modernity became transformed immediately into conservative attitudes and, in the case of Pound, into fascist attitudes. Although Williams's vision is not optimistic either—how could it be?—it does not have reminiscences of other ages. This, which could be an advantage, is really a disadvantage: Williams does not have a philosophical or religious system, a coherent sum total of ideas and beliefs. The one that was offered him by the immediate tradition (Whitman) was unusable. There is a kind of vacuum at the center of the concept of Williams (not in his short poems) which is the very vacuum of contemporary American culture. The Christianity of *The Waste Land* is a burnt, blackened truth, one which will not, in my opinion, flourish again, but it was a central truth and one which, like the light of a dead star, still *touches* us. I find nothing similar in *Paterson*. The comparison with the *Cantos* is no more favorable to Williams. The United States is an imperial power, and if Pound could not be its Vergil he was at least its Milton: his theme is the fall of a great power. The United States conquered the world but lost its soul, its future—that universal future in which Whitman believed. Perhaps because of his very integrity and decency, Williams did not see the imperial side of his country, its demoniacal dimension.

*Paterson* does not have the unity of *The Waste Land* or its religious authenticity—although Eliot's religiousness is negative. The *Cantos,* moreover, are a poetry incomparably vaster and richer than that of Williams, one of the few contemporary texts at the height of our terrible epoch. What of it? The greatness of a poet is not measured by the scale but by the intensity and the perfection of his works. Also by his vivacity Williams is the author of the most *vivid* poems in modern North American poetry. Yvor Wintors rightly said: "Herrick is less great than Shakespeare but probably no less fine and he will last as long as Shakespeare. . . . Williams will be almost as indestructible as Herrick; by the end of this century we shall see him and Wallace Stevens recognized as the two best poets of their generation . . ." A prophecy fulfilled before Winters expected. As for his ideas about a New World poetry: is Williams really the most American of the poets of his epoch? I don't know and I don't care about knowing. On the other hand, I do know that he is the freshest and most limpid. As fresh as a stream of brook water, as limpid as that same water in a glass pitcher on a rough wood table in a whitewashed room in Nantucket. Wallace Stevens once called him "a kind of Diogenes of contemporary poetry." His lantern, lit in the brightness of day, is the only little sun that it has. The reflection of the sun and its refutation: that lantern illumines zones forbidden to natural light.

In the summer of 1970, in Churchill College in Cambridge University, I translated ten of Williams's poems. Afterward, during two other flying visits, one in Veracruz and the other in Zihuatanejo, I translated the others. Mine are not literal translations: literalness is not only impossible but reprehensible. Nor are they (far from it!)

recreations: they are approximations and, at times, transpositions. What I most regret is not having found in Spanish a rhythm equivalent to that of Williams. But rather than entangle myself in the endless theme of poetic translation I prefer to tell how I met him. In 1955, if I remember correctly, Donald Allen sent me a translation into English of a poem of mine, "Hymn among Ruins." The translation made a double impression on me: it was a magnificent translation, and the translator was William Carlos Williams. I promised myself a meeting with him, and on one of my visits to New York I asked Donald Allen to take me to visit Williams, as he had taken me before to meet Cummings. One afternoon we visited him in his Rutherford house. He was already half paralyzed. It was a wooden house, which is frequent in the United States, and it was more the house of a doctor than of a writer. I have never met a man less affected. Just the opposite of an oracle. Possessed by poetry, not by his role as a poet. Humor, lack of inhibition, and that refusal to take yourself seriously, a refusal sadly lacking in Latin Americans. In each French, Italian, Spanish, and Latin American author—especially if he is an atheist and a revolutionary—there is a hidden priest; in Americans *democratic* simplicity, understanding, and humanity—in the true sense of the word "democratic"—break the professional shell. It has always astonished me that, in a world of relations as tough as in that of the United States, cordiality should constantly burst forth like water from an inextinguishable fountain. Perhaps it is due to the religious origins of the American democracy, which was the transposition of the religious community to the political sphere and from the enclosed space of the temple to the open space of the public square. Protestant religious democracy preceded political democracy. The opposite was true among us: democracy was in its origins antireligious and from the beginning it did not tend to fortify society facing the government but to fortify the government facing the Church.

Williams was less loquacious than Cummings, and his conversation made one want to love him more than admire him. We talked about Mexico and the United States. Naturally we fell into the theme of roots. We, I said to him, are choked by the profusion of roots and pasts, but you are overwhelmed by the enormous weight of the crumbling future. He agreed and he gave me a pamphlet just published by a young poet with a prologue that he had written: it was Allen Ginsberg's *Howl.* I saw him again years later, shortly before his death. Although illness had beaten him down cruelly, he kept his temper and his head intact. We spoke again of the three or four or seven Americas: the red, the white, the black, the green, the purple . . . Flossie, his wife, was with us. While we talked I thought of "Asphodel," his great poem of love in old age. Now, recalling that conversation and writing these lines, I mentally cut the colorless flower and breathe its odor. "A curious odor," says the poet, "a *moral* odor." It's not really an odor, "except for the imagination." Isn't that the best definition of poetry: a language that says nothing, except to the imagination? In another poem he compares his poetry with a flower, "Saxifrage, that breaks the rocks." Imaginary flowers that operate on reality, instant bridges between men and things. And so the poet makes the world livable.

# ODE

GUSTAF SOBIN

*for Charles Tomlinson*

1
were saying these things to    stop them,

to keep them / from
being said by    the ceaseless (the un-

sayable).


      •


held, holding them: the breath's gold:
Rembrandt's

black
elephants. because luminous    is
what we've learnt / to darken    (to
circumscribe) with sound:        hoop
to this
circus
of    inversions.


      •

images. tokens and
images:

all   we know; that we'll ever   know of
ourselves. im-

prints of an
obliterating
as-
cendancy (fingers
poking

over the coils / of the fuming kelp).

·

what
we call holiest
goes under. whatever's
ours is

only ours
against.

crypts
of whispers;
mud-
hovels (the white   chords
hoarded); all
our bright-winged   demons
ballasted
in blood.


2
all   we know; that we'll ever   know. . . .

but the flare, the
clamoring

flue of
the
limbs, up-
wards. . . . lovelier
than anything
we've    ever known. the    lessening
into immensity. the spreading    trees
of the instants
in bud. each worded    circle, re-

lapsing, trans-
lucent, into the    eye-
alleviant
of loss.

                    .

we'll never / say
what        we'd say. the jealous soil, its
syntax,
keeps us doubled to    our-
selves. a voice-net

shrivels us
in its    chimeras.
but the sense,
forever,
swells outwards. the null,
sumptuous, draws    at the divided voice.

hear the
intervals
as they pour through the    comb of their
octaves; and the    words,
boned
of all / but their    breath,
spread
radiant!

                    .

was why
he    turned. why

startled, out-
raged, she stopped. and felt her    rip-
pling tall-hipped body
dissolve
to a
word.

wings.

wings! all we have / instead of wings!

# SELECTIONS FROM
# LETTERS TO FRIENDS

PAULA EIGENFELD

*Introduced by John Hawkes*


INTRODUCTORY NOTE

*John Hawkes*

At the end of her third year at Brown University, Paula Eigenfeld was intensely committed to such diverse areas of work as jurisprudence and semiotic approaches to literature. For her, reading was a kind of innocent hunger profoundly felt and repeatedly satisfied by works ranging from Hannah Green's *I Never Promised You a Rose Garden* to the letters of Rilke. She was an almost severely studious person, yet never totally accepted what she called "my intelligence"; she wanted to become a psychiatric social worker, yet assumed, because of her own past hospitalization, that this career was closed to her; she wanted a life of playful, loving relationships, yet considered herself excluded from the ordinariness of daily life which others took for granted but which to her was a form of exalted existence. Most of all, she thought of herself as a writer, and it was in her writing that she was at last clearly and remarkably herself. In her few years at college her love of language increasingly took the form of letters, which became voluminous. Her letters were gifts to others; to herself, in the copies she kept, her letters were an endlessly repeatable form of the life she loved, the life she could not have, the life she feared. In the four months preceding her death, she wrote over three hundred manuscript pages of letters, from which the following brief selection was made. She committed suicide in October of 1976.


1

Someone once told me that I was a "late bloomer." Isn't it yet time for me to "bloom"? But maybe in some ways I *am* blooming now, after all.

In the tenth grade I went out on one date. The guy—no, we all said "boy" then—was big, broad shouldered, and something of a social misfit. He wore high, laced leather shoes in a shade of tan which approached orange. They were big shoes: everyone made fun of them in class, and even I called them "clodhoppers." He had a big head, a long face, dark skin, large sunken brown eyes, very black hair, straight; he was Jewish. The nickname that he went by and which everyone used was Skip; but everyone also knew that his real name was Irving. He was sloppy and not attractive. The reason I went out with him once was partly because he asked me, and partly because he was brilliant and showed some talent in expressive writing. Even in tenth grade, I remembered an oral report that he had given in sixth grade on the subject of the human brain. It was a magnificent report, and I admired his brilliance.

To my disappointment, instead of "going out" on a normal date like everyone else did, we merely took a long walk on a cool spring afternoon. But we went into a church; that was nice. Skip talked about his father, who had died when Skip was little, and whom he seemed to both admire and hate. Anyway (if I remember correctly), Skip felt that I was not sufficiently understanding, or else was too pitying, and therefore ended our date early. I was not physically attracted to him and in fact felt that he was too messy-looking; but I would have liked him to kiss me anyway, especially in the warm dim church.

2

Please, please, leave me alone. Forget about me; it will be easy. You still have a chance to dump me into a garbage can before it is too late; before you yourself are corroded or even infected.

And yet there is another part of me—irrational, and refusing to learn. I am a lonely and deformed child standing in the center of a darkened and whirling nightmare. Standing in the darkness, mutely I stretch, reach toward you and hope that you will take both my hands in yours. I want you to stop this dizziness; make the dark room stop spinning. Hold me. Help me before I destroy myself.

3

The child in me leaps out, and (unknown to anyone), for a few seconds, I am very "regressed": a totally abandoned and hopeless child who is experiencing all the despair of separation and loss. But if one of you stays with me long enough, which means another few seconds, that child becomes able to accept the warmth and comfort and reassurance that are offered, and the fragmented child is calmed and healed before disappearing into me again. It is as though the child has to be recognized and has to be allowed to come to the surface and to experience (within the span of sixty seconds) anguish, loneliness, warmth, and comfort, before being soothed and then reintegrated.

4

Remember that a child needs to be nurtured in order to grow; and a deprived and deformed child—a needful child—needs nurturance because of a drive to grow up and become whole again. Sometimes a child can grow up and be transformed into a writer and even into an adult woman. Am I saying, for the first time, that I want to be nurtured not only so that the child in me can be given milk and then feel somnolent, having a brief rest before waking up to needfulness and drivenness again; but also because that child is finally ready to grow up, *wants* to grow up, and if nurtured, may even be able to change and mature? Yes.

5

It is late at night. I feel as though I have been standing on a mountain peak, at dizzying heights, and also at the edge of a precipice.

It is as though I was given a stimulant drug or hallucinogen and was acting out seductive and beautiful, but dangerous dreams, while entranced. It scares me to hear the affirmations I made, because I know that the world created by those affirmations isn't possible for me. I'll only be hurt, shattered, if I try to follow such visions. Because the real, mundane world for me is one of psychopathology. I know now that I will be granted occasional moments of happiness, communion—even exuberance, transcendence. But most of my existence consists of failure, drivenness, aloneness, self-abuse, neurotic rituals, suffering, and even crying undetected by others . . . The enigma is whether I will continue to destroy myself gradually or will eventually be able to do it abruptly, all at once, achieving release—obliteration.

6

Oh, how warm and good I feel when I am with you, and we talk about writing, language, our lives. I am even starting to relax sometimes; have you noticed? It is strange. I laughed when you described how, as a child, you were dressed up "like an elf." I wasn't laughing at you, but at the humorous picture you created. Even now, I am chortling and spitting on the typewriter keys. An elf! You must admit that is humorous. I do feel sorry for you, though. Although I was never a little boy who had to cope with the dangers of being "feminized," I can accept and empathize with the embarrassment—"the indignity of childhood."

7

You can see that I'm returning to my usual tone of dry self-condemnation . . . But despite the familiar tone, which may be boring to you, real emotions have been stirred. Actually I am struggling against you. I am fighting you as hard as I can, with determination. I am like my mother in having a tremendous amount of energy and stubbornness, and much of that fierce energy I am channeling into my struggle with you. There is nothing amusing about my fighting you. The summer, the future is rushing toward me . . .

But a small part of my energy has been enlisted on your side. Part of me is already aligned with you . . .

8

Do you remember that during our meeting yesterday afternoon—a meeting that already seems to be long ago—at one point, you described me. You strung together a whole list of adjectives, each one strong and positive; you listed these qualities as though you were stringing pearls. And they all referred to me. You were telling me how you see me. Even as you said the words, I was so dazzled by their brightness and heat that I could not really hold and assimilate them. I wanted to ask you to slow down, so that I could hear each word separately. I wanted to hold each pearl in my hand and become acquainted with it.

Now, a mere one day later, I remember only one of the six or eight adjectives that you used. The one that I remember is, of course, "intelligent." It is amazing that out of a string of warm, smooth, hard white words, the only word I remembered is the one that means least to me; the one that has caused me pain in the past. Intelligence. But I know that you said other words, also. You gave me a more complete name.

Now I wish we could have tape-recorded our conversation. I wish I could have written down the positive words you used to describe me. Then I could have looked at the list once after you left me.

Do I really want that list? A list of positive words referring to myself, giving me permission to live, and creating me as a person—a real person. Such a list would confront me with something dazzling and painful, something I can't even name.

Yes, I do. Yes, now I would accept that list.

## 9

I thought that "getting better" would be like being fed; the problem was that no one would ever give me milk. Now I see that another problem is that my system is not equipped to digest milk. My vision has been distorted; the purest nutriment often appears to be a dangerous poison, and my digestive system reacts accordingly. I will have to relax and let go and allow the natural process of feeding and digestion to revive and nurture me. Meanwhile, I seem to be thrashing and fighting.

What is going to happen to me?

## 10

Maybe I have the capacity to smile, to be (occasionally) warm, sunny, expansive, open. You coaxed that potential "good self" to the surface and encouraged it. Wanting to make you aware of this, I spoke, I showed you; I said: "Look; I'm real. I'm whole."

You replied: "Yes, I will accept that; it's good."

You were "naming" me on a profound level then, naming me a person, naming me as someone who can communicate in writing, who can create pleasure for other people as well as creating pain and disappointment, who is capable of deep feeling and mutuality. You were letting me know that it was all right to trust you. You were saying that it is okay for me to exist; I have a right to exist.

11

There is nothing to say about pain, except that it often seems to be self-perpetuating. There is nothing to say about being depressed, except that it is exhausting. I feel dry and scraped out. And there is nothing to say about apprehension and the quicksand of discouragement and hopelessness, except that the sandy vortex into which I'm sinking is located far from where anyone can reach me to pull me out, or far from where many people would try.

12

This year, too, I've especially noticed the massing of people at one service after another. From diverse lives, diverse beliefs, and lack of beliefs, people, even in this day and age, even right here at the University, still come together and somehow simply by appearing in a room or a temple, all are acknowledging the significance of the holidays and of observance—no matter what other claims crowd their lives. Isn't there a kind of reverence in this acknowledgment? And why is it that "Jews," even those who are neither observant nor believers, feel compelled to go to services on these days? Is there something vital in the Jewish tradition? I think there is. And if there is, is any of that vitality available for me to use without hypocrisy or pretense? Maybe.

13

Holding a two-year-old child in my arms, hoisting him high, clasping him against my chest and shoulder, while he wails in sleepy and half-hearted protest. An amazing sense of power and responsibility, born of the knowledge that I am picking up and holding a whole human being, and this small person is unthinkingly trusting. An unexplained feeling of warmth and care.

14

. . . Because being held and cuddled means being protected, loved, accepted, and cherished. It means being less fragile. It means being stronger and whole and accepting, because when you are secure and held in that kind of gentleness, not everything big and small can smash you to pieces. You are a little safer from explosions and implosions.

It is as though someone were saying to you, "I don't hate you. You're not a lousy good-for-nothing to me. I don't think you're no-good. Oh, you're all right, you're all right. I like you. I love you. I am not afraid to touch you or be close to you; there is no stench coming from you now. Quiet, my loved one; be quiet; you can have peace now, you are all right. I don't hate you any more. I don't hate you at all. I don't only care about you, I care for you and have affection for you as a person. I don't hate you; I'm not even angry at you; I don't want to destroy you. I don't wish you would disappear or somehow vanish. I really want you alive."

# TEN POEMS

MARCO ANTONIO MONTES DE OCA

*Translated from the Spanish by Laura Villaseñor*


## I SPEAK WITH YOU

> *For my mother, Mercedes Fernández, widow*
> *of Montes de Oca, on the first anniversary of*
> *her death*

I touch the tiger's stripes
Just like a warm harp
But then my blood
Puts on new wings
And livid flies to the perch
Where the memory of you hangs
Faraway mother mine.

I circle myself without finding me
I flame little but burn too much
Among castles
That growing younger return
To the blond moment
When they were three stones old.

From tumble to tumble
From tomb to tomb
Your arms I seek
Not knowing where you are
And then earth dwindles to
The immensity of your lap
To features painted on snowmen
To ways to walk on a sword's edge
Or to lie down never to live.

Again I go to school
With your picture under my arm
Again I greet the teacher
With a sticky hand
And everyone hits me
Even threats from afar
Of your fistful of doves.

The rain of rice
The sabers crossed above the happy pair
The white cake
The tin cans tied to the wedding car
Have outdistanced the urge to laugh
And only black celebrations
Black weddings of stone with mud
Make the crowds hoarse
In whose breast nostalgia roars.

The sun rises however it can
It stretches and crawls out of bed
Only to hide again
There is not a pore of my body where you do not hurt
And what a face I wear to the office
With what a fluttering pulse
I stamp the card and hurry back
So that no one should smile at me
Quickly limping
To my hole flooded by your absence.

Indeed you went away entirely
Your voice left and your hair
White virgin sand
Now suffers the amnesia of your footprints
Absolutely nothing did you leave me
Only your planetary absence
Only the dust that masks my face
And the reason why my tears fall
Tracing devout highways.

Faraway mother mine
How Africa grows
Now that I am lost
Something that splits lightning has split me
Apollo goes mad behind a mask of bees
And the itch to die thickens like never before
And it drops me and spills me
Like an egg on the tiles.

O dark-green cypresses
O arrows those too-thin birds
O dreams that are the proof
The black-and-blue testimony
Of the innumerable roads
By which desire enters failure:

Again I am the child
Hands and feet wrinkled
From being so long in the dazzled water
And here it is that the voice hoarsens
Repeating your name all year long
And howling with parched throat
When your dress comes back from the garden
With no one inside.

Funereally and forever I am in the air
I open my eyes
With a leaden paperweight
Tied to my eyelashes
And instantly grow numb

And then I freeze
O earth of the new-born fawn
Spotted with coins of snow
Sweet wound on the surface of the petal
Well-sifted golden flour
Inexpressible mother mine.

Rest in my peace that you took away
Fly but come back
Come back but fly
Between slopes where wheat prays crestfallen.

Move as a fountain moves
Sing in honor of the stone mermaids
There below among the waters blindly entwining
Blow bubbles of sparkling silver
On the alabaster flute.

It's enough to see inside me
To know you are not gone
Enough to see the stone niche
To know you do not fit there:
I am who holds you
And carries you everywhere
Like a living palanquin
A barefoot wave
A monstrance that yellows on touching you
And grows and bristles its reflections
Like the head of an electrified lion.

I am who bathes you with splendors
Of a dying emerald
It is I
And the throat of the hero
And the islands of piled salt
Who leave you on the blind threshold
While the heart offers
To beat easily for us both.

Regicide is always possible
To hate life
But the conjurors
The daring exorcists
Do not know that you have gone not to leave
They do not know that before setting out
You were already back
They do not know as they should
That your whereabouts cannot be traced
Because you were never lost.

I speak with you as if I had died
I speak with you and fall sick
Not understanding
Why they say you are dead
If really you are with me
*Faraway mother mine.*


## ELEGY OF HOMECOMING

Ah, subtle song, sob of ocarina,
You pass between stills or drums
Like a slenderest serpent
And do not stop, you shatter the sluice
You follow your way
Never once stumbling,
Always surer and more winged at each step!

Because of you I linger in the ended exile
And delay indefinitely the visit to my parents,
Those who wait for me
With a splendid spray of teeth in the mouth,
Totally smiling,
Quite in love with the air
That their small prodigal son breathes.

I stay a bit longer at home.
I press myself into the loving south,
Into the friendship of strange plants that easily hold me
On their golden stem.
I want to stay another century in my blue labyrinth
To contemplate the circle of the inflamed celebrants
Like the sweetest conspiracy
Never before invented against my head's aberrations.

Shy clarity, paradise in readiness,
Slightest reed,
Will you arise when the wind falls
To the point of intersection
Where the wave and the moon at last kiss?
Hymn of the master for the slave,
High river of sleepwalking doves,
Do not put me more adrift:
Look how my root misses me
And all you need do is interrupt my flight
And let me fall into it.

Hail, salve, good day!
Hello, crystal field,
Strong wine that bleeds
Among the thousand cunning clefts of my returning soul!

Hardly has this red splendor passed
That absorbs my senses
This happiness free of pronouns,
These heartbeats that weep springtimes;
I shall return, O God, I shall return
To the unique arms
That tied me to the world.

## MOVEMENT IS PERPETUAL AS LONG AS IT LASTS

The past does not die with the dead
Here it is mired but moving
Hypnotized wheel
Red scattered homily
Under the hissing water
Carrousel that girds me
Like a coat of cut glass:
This is the rendezvous
This is the encounter.

## LOGS FOR THE SAME FIRE

Everything all shes all hes
Will now want to move more in less space
And the eye itself must prepare
To jump the rope of the eyebrow.

We shall be careful to sharpen the castles
And to keep what concerns only a few:
            Unearthing of the earth
            Unearthing of language
            Slow unearthing of violets
            That fly faster than their aroma:
            Eternity is made
            Of the moments I forgot to live.

## ALIVE AND STILL LIFE

I draw a halo around the apple
But better I'll taste the worm
Clean sound svelte
Corrupting and not corrupt:
Only the apple
Is rotten.

# THE WINDOWS MUST BE OPENED

Great wings cover beggars on the corners
Oceans of green eyes
Float without touching sand;
Beneath the rocks images awake
At the stroke of a fan
And that is good
For us who are alive
And need a sign to know it.

The river watches the city pass by
The closed fist is an open dahlia;
Eleven children playing
Gather round a derelict motor
And loosen the bursting reveille
Where the ground grows
Toward the farthest echo.

I no longer ask which hole of nothingness is mine
I hear what a lily says,
Dim loudspeaker of silk
That lights silence and spreads it.

I open the curtains
I break the blinds of my room into a thousand sparrows
As now fervor flings wounds instead of thunderbolts
And insomnia is chased down the corridors
With a fevered torch.

The mighty green of the beloved earth
Kindles in unison
Nature without and within.

## ADVICE TO A SHY GIRL OR IN DEFENSE OF A STYLE

> Man be my metaphor
> —Dylan Thomas

I like to beat about the bush. There is no better way
to arrive to the top of the tree. If that weren't
enough, a straight line sickens me; I prefer a fizzing
squib and its feverish zigzag flowered with lights.
And when I dream, I see frontón courts gorged with jewels
where vegetations of lightning last until I thread
them with iridescent shells in the deepest glee. To
the devil with scanty ornament and the austere norms
with which academies prune the splendor of the world!

And you, my girl, don't come tonight with a frugal
little ribbon at the waist and naked hands. I want to
see on the luxuriant cascade of your hair that tiara of
green eyes that I stole for you when pillage and in-
justice tyrannized my senses and erected fanfares of
scandal in the charnel house. Dare to come dressed in
exultation and summer. And if, thinking of the risks,
you are worried, pay no attention: lose yourself in cavil-
ing over the intimate structure of Andromeda. Raise the
collar of your coat. Look up and down like a disdainful
star. And when we are outside, far from this meeting
of castrated notaries, when your train of broken
dishes has burst their delicate eardrums, you and I
will delight like no one before in a cluster of wild
flowers.

## ADRIFT

*For Eduardo and Laura Villaseñor*

The ship its own port
Has nowhere to go
Wandering Jew among the waters
Small vessel in which eternity rains

If you take me here I'll go there
If you say stay I'll sail on
My contradictory spirit
Is as large at least
As your freedom
Great art says nothing
If it is neither here nor there
I don't want to be taken away
Nor to be nailed in one spot
Waves cover me
But the wave has not been born
That should drown me
O eagles my love is greater
Than the space you have ploughed
But always quiet
Close to the hearth
Facing the eternal bubbles of the stars
Being at once port and ship
I would rather neither arrive nor leave
I would rather say that trees own the silence
Though without light
They have never been much.


APPEARANCE

Spider of sadness
Turbulent wave
Bury me inside the poem
But with one arm left above
So I cannot forget
The wind that forgets me.

We who have always been alone
Thank dream for its appearance
Its scourge does not hurt but ravishes
Just as a wild animal barely clawing
        barely kills
Memory murders better
When it asks
Why we go on living.

Bury me O friendly birds
With one arm above the earth:
When the wind dies
Forgetfulness will be reborn.


## AN AFTERNOON IN EASY PAYMENTS

Here there is a fluff of thistledown enchanted to know me
To know me
        and the dusty ostrich
                and the grown-up chick
Among swans that pretend to be paper boats
Paper boats that pretend to go on swimming
And oars
      Silken anchors
              in place of a necktie
Fancies of nature and loosened marvels
Filth and accumulations
In a meter of air that is no-man's-land
Or the flower that becomes the scream of its color
Yellow
      Violet
        Black
A fierce orange that eats whoever looks at it
And that howls as if light's feet had been trampled
Quickening its vigor winded
By the silence that did not mount its throne
By the light before the first light
And when the jerk of departure
That the sky-rocket gives
In its double hunger of death and sky
Begins to clamor its half-closed work
With the trill that cracks the jar
With the volume of what is sung
The cipher
      The violence
          The finale

That moment when reality knows
That if I am not aware of it
It cannot really happen
Not even though its glimmer
Melts the pistil fan of my eyes
Not even though October falls
Ariadne
      And her thread
             The minotaur
                    The labyrinth
Even though everything falls
Except the sky that one way or another
Everyone had believed it possible to fell.

# SNOW AND ICE

CHRISTINE L. HEWITT

"Every form of life is affected differently
by the depth of snow."

"Once snow crystals land on the ground,
they start to lose their fine detail through a
process called metamorphosis or sublima-
tion."—Donald W. Stokes, *A Guide to Na-
ture in Winter*

It was too snowy for me that day. The snowflakes alighted on my
eyeballs and melted and made rivulets of cold water down my
cheeks. He guided me to the midway lodge, and then sped off,
graphing his curves in the snow in tune with the music which he
told me was always in his head. He would gladly forgo the speed
to the pleasure of the powder, that was what he said.

When I woke up today it was with the desire to throw small
breakable objects against the opposite wall. I wanted the music of
their myriad shattering. I thought of the collection of prismatic glass
animals left to him by his grandmother, now left to me. Where are
they now, when I need them?

I watched him wrestle with the bulldog on the back porch. A
bulldog makes a strange noise when she is laughing. What did I

know? I said to him, Tell me a few parting words. Something to think about for the rest of a lifetime.

He was standing on the threshold of our bedroom, balancing upon that rounded piece of wood, back and forth upon the balls of his feet. I was lying back upon the large bed, my knees held up to my chest and all of me hidden beneath my flannel nightgown. One thing before you leave, I said. One sentence that will repeat itself autonomously in my mind like a song.

There is no heat in my house now. It is past the time of excitement over budding croci. It is beyond April.

This morning, while my hair was wet and tangled after a bout with the shower, I kicked at all the bookcases, and threw all the books onto the floor: thirteen volumes of Edgar Allen Poe, *Scott's Last Expedition,* the uncut works of Camus and Butor, and so on. All day long I could hear the piles of books shifting among themselves and tumbling further down with the inevitable pull of gravity. Now that I write about it, in the dead calm of retrospect, in this retrospection of dead passion, it seems to have been so systematic. I have no system but to get through each day with the minimum of longing.

It has something to do with the giant mice that ran races in the eaves all winter. I will remember what it is with time, with the right stimulus.

I gazed down upon the tarsal bone of my right foot, not a little surprised. In my mind it was swelling to gigantic, mutant proportions. I looked at him, and at his hand so recently emptied of its projectile. "How could you be so vicious?" I asked him.

"If I threw a hardback at your face, that would be vicious," he answered. "A paperback at your foot is hardly vicious."

*Aardvarks to Cyclops,* Volume 1, bounced upon his knees. Beneath the book the muscles of his thighs rose like Indian mounds used for undiscovered religious ceremonies. When I learned that capybaras were not farmyard animals, were not prehistoric creatures, but were the world's largest rodents, I thought it was a very good joke. It had been a long time since he had told me a joke, and I wanted this to be one.

Even when he was outside, when the back door had slammed, and he was beyond the porch, even then I was sure that I could hear his footsteps, crunching dead brush on their way down the hill, squishing into the quickly rising tidal marsh: water in his shoes, water on the knee, water fills the sky if the earth were upside-down. And panting beside me, the bulldog's tongue touched the floor and a puddle grew at the tip of her grainy pink appendage. I pressed a steady hand to Smelly's head, and tried to pace my heartbeat, and hoped that the evenness of my pulse would transmit itself to her. Controlled breathing is very important.

"If you have so much against the horizontal position, let's try it sitting up," he said. He was unbuckling his belt as he spoke.
"Don't talk to me of novelties," I said.
"Are you being prudish, or what?"
"What," I answered. The word came too quickly, like a little porcelain animal falling off a shelf.

It is unseasonable weather I am having. The new buds age quickly. I have not accustomed myself to spring tides, as if I were a foreigner.

"Asia is where all the people are," this is what he said.
"Antarctica is where all the penguins are."
"But we're not going there," he said. "No local source of vegetables."
"Where are we going? I have quite a lot of responsibilities here," I said. He looked around, waiting for them to announce themselves. He saw baby pictures, animal bones upon the mantle, lawn furniture indoors, four or five wastebaskets of crumpled white Kleenex.

I do a little dance on the cold white tiles of the bathroom floor. I watch the coils of the electric heater redden. Once I saw those coils as vessels of passion. Now passion seems to be a vessel that has sailed irrevocably over the horizon.
Often I dream of the floors becoming sheets of ice. I have to skate from room to room.

Weighty silence was a discipline I had to learn, for him. Now it is the texture of mornings, the music of afternoon, the fear in the night.

"In the South, certain women eat dirt when they are pregnant. But in South America, they eat crushed limestone. They receive visions of their future children from it."
I had to ask, "Where did you learn that?"
"In the encyclopedia, under 'Organic Foods.' "
"I read the entire encyclopedia as a child." That is what he always said.

From the broken eggshells at breakfast I learn about the connections between all things in nature, between oyster shells and the carapace of a horseshoe crab and the snail-houses and the stolen penguin eggs.

From week to week, the topography of Antarctica is changed by the ocean currents and undertows, by the crunching and shoving of the ice packs.

The same question in every room of the house: A hint, please? A clue to what I should be thinking from now on? My ear was not subtle enough to catch the echo. I was sure there was an echo.

I can remember sitting in an antiseptic corner of a north country hospital. I watched the parade of ski boots past my huddled form; they trailed in gravelly snow that melted and formed puddles in barely perceptible depressions in the floor. A doctor stroked my hair and gave me a pill. I can remember stroking the elbows of my red-down parka. I remember feeling sure that I had finally rubbed through to the bone.

The din of the tree swallows does not cease. They are as persistent as spring growth. The organization of their music is not orchestral, but natural, like the sound of the glaciers pushing ice into the sea pack, like the squeaking of the ice floes as they crush one another, and all else, natural as the imperceptible waddling of the penguins back to the rookery.

Geography is the study of anything that can be explained or defined on a map. There are many maps tacked up on the walls of this house. There are many more which have fallen down and now gather foreign dust along the plinths. He objected to a sense of visual organization that could only be controlled by thumbtacks.

I race the bulldog down to the marsh, where it is exactly low tide. The dried mud left by the receding sea colors the spartina grass white. This marsh is as solid as a tectonic plate. I cross the channels with a seven-league stride. A pale thin stream of water flows through each muddy ditch, a strange denial to the lunar flood tides, the roar of succeeding oceans. Smelly would like to jump—her flat head descending first—into the slimy channel, and wallow. I must carry her across the gap. I can feel her abdominal muscles, separated from me by her short golden fur, straining against my outstretched hands. We are looking for great blue herons. We have seen the little blues, as they long-leggedly pace the marsh's edge. Most of them have returned from the south by now, from their winter home in selvatic greenery. The great blues feed on small fishes and crabs. I gather those desiccated shells in my hands and they elude me like brittle leaves.

In the cold and arid air, I can remember feeling icicles grow where there once were tonsils.

The rodents are eating the leather bindings of his old textbooks. Sometimes tiny strings, licked clean of glue, leftovers, will litter the bookshelves in the morning. One night I go downstairs and watch the tiny eyes of a mouse, watching me, as it continues to gnaw. I lunge for it with two long arms. Then my fist hits the back of the bookcase and the whole structure falls upon me. I am tangled up in my flannel nightgown. Books I have never opened are falling upon my head. It is very painful, and I remember that I need him to tell me which limb I should straighten first, and which I should bend, and which direction I should aim for, to get out from under.

There is something reassuring in the skeletal structure of ourselves, and of the animals.

Soon after we moved to this house, this swampy outpost, he wanted to make love on the rug in front of the fire. I felt sure that my coccyx was being bruised by its staccato pounding upon the floor, which was separated from my back by this itchy Persian carpet. When the telephone rang he was already asleep. I stood in the kitchen speaking into the receiver, and watched the semen drip along my right thigh and form a small puddle between my bare feet. The linoleum was cold, and I watched the goose bumps with the same diffidence.

He brought me the skull of a fox from the surrounding woods. I remember soaking it in bleach on the back porch, wanting it to be as white as the snow of an avalanche. The smell of the last remnants of rotting flesh drifted in through the cracks in the house, and down the chimney. My hands turned raw and ghostly from the bleach.

Each day on this marsh includes some of the hottest and driest and coldest and wettest of climates. The footprints of camels, bearing picnickers to the pyramid at Giza, are quickly covered by the action of Sahara breezes. The camels sway like the visual wailing of a flute. The footprints of the high-stepping caballos, circling the freshly swept plaza de toros, are as sharp and clear as a wound in the sunlight. Shackleton and his men lived for months on the ice floes of the Weddell Sea, which were constantly melting during the Antarctic summer and were much damaged by the passage of dogs and sledges. The men were never dry, never changed their clothes; they slept in soggy sleeping bags whose linings had mildewed. Their finneskos shed their furry shape, became bald. Yet only two toes were lost to the black and withering frostbite. The men all survived, on seal and penguin meat, and short rations of pemmican. It is a fact that Emperor penguins mate at the height of the winter. Their rookeries are the largest settlements of any kind south of the Antarctic circle.

I pounded upon the bathroom door, to be let in. My knuckles have a low pain threshold. I hollered across the plywood barrier, You can't go without letting me know all the things I have to know. Aren't I your responsibility? I wouldn't ask if I didn't need to know.

It was not what I felt like doing very often that winter, beneath those complicated layers of clothes.

I told him how I had dreamt of Robert Falcon Scott, the last to die of starvation and cold in their snow-covered tent; how instead of writing those last messages with a pen, the ink had flowed from his own frozen fingertips. "Have you ever heard this syntax before?" I asked him. He was trying to extract from beneath my head the four pillows that I had accumulated during the night. I read: " 'Had we lived, I should have had a great tale to tell . . .' " But I began to weep instead of finishing the sentence.

"What does it mean to be so easily provoked to tears?" he asked. "Me? I should be asking you," I said. And he looked as if he knew the answer.

I can hear the mice running relay races between the walls. They are wearing little numbered vests made from all my lost handkerchiefs. They defy me. I leave no food out for them, but they leave me pellets in the napkin drawer. I am incommunicado and they do not care.

I told him that I could remember when prehistoric animals roamed across this hill, when they lumbered through and crushed the accumulated leaves of autumns. I described them as giant, mutant bulldogs. He believed me, and asked for details.

One day I put my hand through the kitchen window; I want to feel the unfamiliar sunshine on my knuckles. The glass falls about my arm like crushed ice.

Did he find me unresponsive? Did he ever complain? In my mind, I was beating his back with closed fists, demanding, demanding. He always insisted on nakedness and I remember touching the soles of my chilly feet to his thighs.

I was eating breakfast, reading a magazine, picking dead leaves from a common houseplant. His was a body already on its way to work. I said, The words of wisdom, please? Something to illuminate the rest of life for me, or I shall never be able to think in sentences again.

It is the season of tender, moist glasswort. I lie back upon the low-tide marshlands, and pluck out their pink, translucent network of roots with my hands. Smelly barks from a distance, but will not come near me when I am horizontal, and obsessed, so she thinks.

The camera stood upon its tripod, and he was focusing its lens upon the migrating Canada geese. I was wrapped in a blanket, standing at the door to the back porch. He had not spoken to me all morning, would not wipe away my tears. I watched the steadiness of his hand. I knew *I* could never make it shake. I asked, Isn't there something you want to tell me? Before it can never be said again? Listen. "I am as quiet as a mouse."

He photographed my instep, my breasts, my profile, a hundred times. Sometimes I look at the test strips, to look through his eyes. It is no use. We had different degrees of vision.

I photographed him once, beside a pyramid. He was wearing khaki pants, a blue polo shirt, and hiking boots. He was explaining to me how to use the light meter, because the sunshine enveloped us. The photograph, as he developed it, came out both light and dark.

He wanted me to perform unnatural acts. I pounded my head against the wooden bedboard, to demonstrate my invincible stubbornness. He told me that it was all right, that he would bring me aspirin. "Where did you learn that word 'unnatural'?" he asked.

"I've always known it," I answered.

It is springtime and I remember snowfalls. Today I know two things: silence and connections. Snow covers the marsh like gauze and is merged with the ocean when the tide rises. The snow's weight has no effect upon the spartina grass; not like the wind, the ruffled surfaces. All the earth's crust is made rough and uneven by the shifting of tectonic plates, like an amusement park gone haywire.

He covered my mouth with his hand. "You're always telling me, telling me things," he said.

"Don't you want to know how I yearned secretly for you from an early age? That I have *always* loved you?" I had said this so many times. I never knew whether he believed it or not.

"I don't want to know," he said, and that was what I expected. We were beneath the heavy Mexican blankets, arranging our pillows for the long wintry night.

"How can I sleep with someone who's a mystery to me?" I demanded. Nonetheless, we made love that night. I bit the pillows, because he did not like me to bite his shoulders, although I had never drawn blood.

One of Robert Falcon Scott's companions, Evans, went outside the tent into a blizzard, a raging blizzard. He was found over a mile away, "on his knees with clothing disarranged, hands uncovered and frostbitten, and a wild look in his eyes." Evans died soon after he was discovered. Scott wrote his widow a moving letter as he sat in his enshrouded tent, waiting to make a widow of another faithful wife.

The tracks of the dinosaurs led right up to the house, but there were no signs of damage. I wanted to touch their scaly skin, or climb their horny backs. He made me sit at the breakfast table until all the food was gone. He told me to stay off the marsh when the water was rising, to stay out of the woods when the rodents were mating, to stay out of the town during rush hour. I let him stroke my head. Inside the skull pocket it sounded to me like the crackling of old yellow paper, from unread books.

"I don't want a token, I want the real thing," I shouted, my hands extended, my mouth open, for anything I could get.

Soon there will be lilacs, pale lavender flowerlets, bushes like clouds. Lilacs are like him, sweet-smelling and fleeting.

Mallory and Oates and Scott died the slow cold death.

Will I turn yellow in this new untempered sunshine?

He skied off a ledge. He landed one hundred feet below in a snow and rock filled ravine. After climbing down an avalanche-posted mountainside through waist-high snow, the ski patrol found him. His neck was cleanly broken. He was the most wonderful skier I ever knew. That is a fact to me, just like his death. All that winter I mourned him with one picture in my mind: of him, cutting those swaths in the new powder and the snow rising all around him like a circumferential wake. How he loved the powder, as if it had a body of its own. It was too snowy for me that day. The snowflakes alighted on my eyeballs and melted and made rivulets of cold water down my cheeks. He guided me to the midway lodge, and then sped off, graphing his curves in the snow in tune with the music which he told me was always in his head. He would gladly forgo speed to the pleasure of the powder, that was what he said. Could he feel the crystals melting on his tongue—his astonished open mouth—as he skied over air? Could he see the edge? Could he discern the exact moment when there ceased to be solid earth beneath his fiber glass skis, his plastic and foam boots, his nylon and down clothing, his body? Could he have imagined himself to be weightless?

All those questions I have still to ask.

# FOUR POEMS

GERARD MALANGA

*ANAKÉ,* WHICH MEANS FATE

A place
to come back to
always

in the mind

one table
chair

with a shirt
now hanging in front of it

stomach   hair   breast

curled up
in a kind of
close breathing

there is a time
elsewhere

disappearing

one window
adjacent to
the bed

the light
coming in

quietly

a dog
barking


THE KENTUCKY DERBY

Love turns to hate
and hate
poisons the heart
the fact

        •

Time
tearing itself
apart

        •

What did you
come away with

        •

the relationship:

"a short
history
of decay"

is what
you made
of it

     •

the distant past
becomes more
distant, still

     •

Your fears
have made you
stupid

## THIS WILL KILL THAT

> Thyself thou gav'st, thy own worth then not knowing,
> Or me, to whom thou gav'st it, else mistaking
> —Sonnett LXXXVII, Shakespeare

A form of words takes shape
but it in itself
is not complete

not simply given—

wants to say more
in saying less

proves nothing—

is of no help to me


what words—ennui, acedia

doubt

decomposition

the infinity
of death

not *we*
but a vital singularity


How shall one
say it,

*how dear*
*you are*
*to me*

*that you*
*alone are you*

a lovely
dignity

tenderness
disclosed as beauty

I keep coming back to you
in my mind

I want to kill this feeling in me
before it kills me
before it gets to me first

a walk of
half an hour
or so
thru city streets

one place in mind

all night awake

eyes   noses   feet

the alarm
clock
goes off

You get up to
turn it off

and then go off

to sleep
again

night
comes
to
an end,
always

&bull;

What is this fear of
unequivocal involvement

why the death of something now

why not later

Why not never

You
are
a pleasure

all ways

like they say


again
and
again
and
again

●

"A Short
History
of Decay"


Think of the
implications

So much
has gone
away

Let's not
let it

Let it be otherwise

Let not the last time
be the first

Place it,
make a space
for it
        authentically

one heart    one mind

It is now, of course, years later

## LITTLE  ITALY

Thinking last night
capuccino    espresso

a walk thru dark streets
1    2    4:30 AM

time
tearing itself
apart

eyes fall to sleep

one mind one heart
at least

the city is waking

my own
sense of it, at least

Someone I've always
wanted to be—
me

seeing the girl
to the door

# NOTES ON CONTRIBUTORS

LINSEY ABRAMS is a graduate of Sarah Lawrence College and the master's program in creative writing at the City College of New York, where she was a fellow in 1976–77 and the recipient of the Jerome Lowell DeJur Award for a series of short stories entitled "Angela En Route." She lives in New York City.

Information on BREYTEN BREYTENBACH can be found in the translator's note introducing his "Five Poems." DENIS HIRSON was born in South Africa, where his father was a political prisoner, and now lives in Paris, working with a theater group and teaching English. His translations of poetry and short stories by Breytenbach will be published this spring by John Calder, Ltd. (London).

COLEMAN DOWELL'S fourth novel *Too Much Flesh and Jabez,* was brought out last year by New Directions. His other books include *Island People* (1976) and *Mrs. October Was Here* (1974), both with ND, and *One of the Children Is Crying* (Random House, 1968). A native Kentuckian, he now makes New York City his home.

Thoughts about PAULA EIGENFELD will be found in JOHN HAWKES's introduction to "Selections from Letters to Friends." Hawkes himself has recently been the subject of a new series of ND publications, *Insights: Working Papers in Contemporary Criticism. A John Hawkes Symposium: Design and Debris* was published in the fall of 1977.

ALLEN GINSBERG'S recent publications include *First Blues: Rags, Ballads & Harmonium Songs* (Full Court Press, 1975), *Journals: Early Fifties, Early Sixties* (Grove Press, 1977), and *Mind Breaths, Poems 1972–1977* (City Lights, 1977). A recording of *First Blues* is now in preparation, produced by John Hammond, Sr., as well as *Mantra & Poetics: 1975–1978,* to be published by Grey Fox Press.

PETER GLASSGOLD assures readers of these pages that "The Third Eye of a Bodhisattva" is not to be taken as the definitive word on either the Aquarian Age or urban American moral decay. His colleagues agree, slyly subtitling the story among themselves as "An Editor's Revenge."

Born in Budapest in 1929, GÁBOR GÖRGEY has become one of Hungary's leading contemporary poets and playwrights. "Interview" is from *Köszönöm, Jól ("I'm Fine Thanks,"* 1970) his third book of poetry. JASCHA KESSLER, himself a poet, playwright, and fiction writer, teaches English at the University of California at Los Angeles.

A versatile writer living in the Bay Area of California, BOBBIE LOUISE HAWKINS has also worked as actress and artist-illustrator. She has published two books of poetry (*Own Your Body,* Black Sparrow, and *Fifteen Poems,* Arif Press), one of short stories (*Frenchy and Cuban Pete,* Timbouctou Press), and a novel (*Back to Texas,* Bear Hug Press). She is now putting together a cycle of one-act plays with music to be called *Closed-Circuit: An American Amusement.* Last winter, Ms. Hawkins was poet-in-residence at New College in San Francisco.

Educated in Egypt, Massachusetts, and California, CHRISTINE LEHNER HEWITT has had two stories published in *The North American Review* and is currently working on a novel, tentatively titled *Confession of the Elder Sister.*

SHERRIL JAFFE was born in 1945 in Walla Walla, Washington, raised in Beverly Hills, attended the University of California at Berkeley, and has since moved to Sebastopol, California. She is the author of *Scars Make Your Body More Interesting* (Black Sparrow, 1975). "Hawaii" is from *This Flower Only Blooms Every Hundred Years,* a novel in progress.

A contributor to *ND27* and *ND33,* RÜDIGER KREMER is a poet, novelist, radio-playwright and has worked as an editor for Radio-Bremen, West Germany. "Love Poem" is translated by BREON MITCHELL, whose *James Joyce and the German Novel* was published in 1976 by Ohio University Press.

GERARD MALANGA is the author of several books of poetry, most recently *Rosebud* (Penmaen Press) and *Ten Years After* (Black Sparrow). The poems published here are part of a work in progress, *This Will Kill That*. Malanga lives in New York and works as a photographer.

The Mexican poet MARCO ANTONIO MONTES DE OCA has published eight books of his poetry and has been the recipient of various fellowships, including a Guggenheim in 1967–68 and again in 1970–71. LAURA VILLASEÑOR is a resident of Mexico City. Her translation of "Piedra de Sol" by Octavio Paz appeared in *The Texas Quarterly*.

Mexico's most distinguished living poet and essayist, OCTAVIO PAZ, was born in 1914. His books with New Directions include *Configurations, Early Poems 1935–1955*, and *Eagle or Sun?* DONALD WALSH has translated a number of Spanish-American poets for ND, among them Ernesto Cardenal's *Apocalypse and Other Poems*, which he co-edited with Robert Pring-Mill.

A regular contributor to these pages, JAMES PURDY's recent collection of stories and plays, *A Day After the Fair*, was brought out in 1977 by Five Trees Press. "How I Became a Shadow" is excerpted from his forthcoming novel *Narrow Rooms*, to be published this year by Arbor House.

GEOFFREY RIPS is a native of San Antonio, Texas, now living in New York. "I Explain Myself" is part of his novel in progress, *The Midwife*.

Biographical information about DELMORE SCHWARTZ is given in JAMES ATLAS's introduction to "Selections from the Verse Journals". Atlas is the author of *Delmore Schwartz: The Life of an American Poet* (Farrar, Straus & Giroux, 1977) and edited the new Schwartz short story collection *In Dreams Begin Responsibilities* published this year by New Directions.

GUSTAF SOBIN was born in Boston in 1935 and graduated from Brown University in 1958. For the past fifteen years he has been living in France, translating from the French and Provençal poetry, film scenarios, and children's books (*The Tale of th*

*Triangle* was published by Braziller in 1973). His first work to appear in the United States, "Seven Poems," was included in *ND32*.

For biographical information on HERMANN TALVIK, see the introduction to his "Eight Drawings" by ALEKSIS RANNIT, curator of Russian and East European studies at Yale University. Rannit has published several monographs on modern artists with UNESCO. His own distinguished poetry has appeared in translation from the original Estonian in earlier ND anthologies.

ANNE WALDMAN is currently living in Nederland, Colorado. Some of her books include: *Giant Night* (Corinth Books), *Life Notes*, (Bobbs-Merrill), and *Fast Speaking Woman* (City Lights). She teaches at the Naropa Institute in Boulder.

Author of more than ten volumes of fiction, criticism, and general prose, PAUL WEST has been a frequent contributor to ND anthologies. *Gala*, his latest book, was published in 1976 by Harper & Row.